Enid Blyton

THE CHILDREN
OF
CHERRY-TREE FARM

First published in 1972
Reprinted in 1983, 1985

Published by Deans International Publishing
52–54 Southwark Street, London SE1 1UA
A Division of The Hamlyn Publishing Group Limited
London · New York · Sydney · Toronto

ISBN 0 603 03289 3

Printed and bound by Purnell and Sons (Book Production) Ltd.,
Paulton, Bristol.
Member of BPCC plc

ENID BLYTON

THE CHILDREN
OF
CHERRY-TREE
FARM

DEANS
INTERNATIONAL
PUBLISHING

CONTENTS

CHAPTER   PAGE

I. A GREAT SURPRISE 7

II. OFF TO CHERRY-TREE FARM 12

III. THE FIRST DAY AT THE FARM 17

IV. THE HUNT FOR THE WILD MAN 23

V. PENNY HAS AN ADVENTURE BY HERSELF. . 32

VI. TAMMYLAN AND HIS CAVE 38

VII. BENJY PAYS A VISIT 44

VIII. TAMMYLAN AND THE SNAKES 51

IX. A MOONLIGHT ADVENTURE. 63

X. TAMMYLAN'S TREE-HOUSE 70

XI. THE VELVET-COATED MINER 77

XII. AN EXCITING MORNING 83

XIII. TAMMYLAN'S SQUIRRELS 91

XIV. BENJY HAS A BIRTHDAY. 98

XV. A NIGHT IN THE TREE-HOUSE 104

XVI. TWO MORE FRIENDS 110

XVII. THE TAIL THAT BROKE OFF 117

XVIII. THE STRANGE FROG-RAIN 126

XIX. FLITTERMOUSE THE BAT 137

XX. PENNY'S PRICKLY PET 145

XXI. THE BATTLE OF THE STAGS 152

XXII. A QUEER PERFORMANCE. 161

XXIII. PRESENTS – AND AN UNEXPECTED VISITOR . 168

XXIV. THE BEST SURPRISE OF ALL! 179

I

A GREAT SURPRISE

One early spring day three children looked out of a window in a tall London house. Below them was a busy street, and not far off was a patch of trees and grass with a tall railing round them.

"The trees aren't even budding yet," said the biggest boy, Rory. He was the oldest of the family, black-haired and brown-eyed. "How I do hate to be in London in the spring-time!"

"Well, we always have been, and I suppose we always shall be," said Sheila. She was twelve, a year younger than Rory. Her hair was fair, but her eyes were as brown as Rory's.

The other boy rested his chin on his hand and looked thoughtfully down at the London square below.

"What are you thinking about, Benjy?" asked Sheila. "Wondering if there are any birds nesting in those trees, I suppose? Or if you might suddenly see a rabbit in the street, or a fox slinking by? You'll have to wait till our summer holidays to see those things."

"I wish we were rich enough to have a cottage in the country, as some people have," said Benjy. "Wouldn't I just love to see all the spring flowers coming out and to watch for frog spawn in the ponds!"

Benjy was ten — a thin, quiet boy who spent all his spare time reading about animals and birds. He was not the youngest; there was Penelope, who was only seven. She was downstairs with her mother, who was bandaging a cut finger for her.

And it was whilst she was there that Penelope heard the Great News. She listened with all her ears whilst the grown-ups were talking; and as soon as her finger was bandaged she flew up the stairs, bursting to tell the news!

She flung open the door, and stood there panting. The others turned round in surprise and saw Penelope's blue eyes shining.

"You'll get into a row if you make such a noise," said Sheila. "You came upstairs like a dozen elephants."

"Rory! Sheila! Benjy! Listen! I've heard something marvellous!" cried Penelope.

"What?" asked the others.

"Well, we're all going down to Cherry-Tree Farm to stay with Auntie Bess for at least six months!" shouted Penelope, and she danced round the table in joy.

"Penny! Are you sure?" cried Rory.

"Oh, Penny! It can't be true!" shrieked Sheila.

"But what about school?" asked Benjy in surprise.

"Mummy said that the doctor advised a good long holiday for all of us," said Penny, still skipping about happily. "She said . . ."

"Penny, do stop still and tell us everything properly," begged Rory. So Penny sat down on a stool and told her brothers and sister what she had heard.

"Well, we've all had measles, and then we had the flu, and then Benjy and I got that awful cough, and Mummy said we were all so thin and pale, and we didn't eat enough, and the doctor said the only thing to do was to let us run wild down in the country, and Mummy said, 'What about Cherry-Tree Farm?' and the doctor said, 'Splendid,' and Daddy said, 'Just the thing,' and I listened and didn't say a word, and . . ."

"Oh, Penny, it's too good to be true!" said Benjy. "No

school! Just going wild in the country. I'd like to go wild. I wish I could go down the rabbit-holes and live wild there. I wish I could get into a hollow tree and live wild there. I wish . . ."

"Benjy, don't be silly! It will be much nicer to live at Cherry-Tree Farm with Auntie Bess and Uncle Tim!" said Rory. "Golly! Cream every day! And those apple-pies with cheese that Auntie Bess makes! And strawberries straight out of the garden! What do people live in a town for?"

"Oh, to ride on buses and go to cinemas, I expect," said Sheila. "When are we going, Penny?"

Penny didn't know any more, but Mother soon came up and told them all about it.

"You go on Thursday," she said. "You have all had

such a lot of illness, so there must be no more school for you for some time. Just the country air and good food and lots of walks. I can't come with you, because Daddy wants me to go to America with him — but Auntie Bess will look after you well."

What an excitement there was for the next two days! The children were given one small trunk between them in which to pack any toys or books they wanted to take with them. Mother packed their clothes, but she said they might pack their toy trunk themselves.

Sheila wanted to take her biggest doll, but Rory would not let her. "It will take up half the trunk," he said. "Take a little one."

Then Penny wanted to take her whole family of golliwogs. She had seven.

"Well, if you take those golliwogs, you can't take anything else at all," said Rory firmly. "Not a thing. No, not even that dreadful rabbit without any ears."

In the end they all took what they wanted most. Rory took pencil-boxes, paint-boxes, and painting-books, for painting was his hobby. Sheila took her work-basket, some puzzles and a small doll. Benjy took nothing but books. Penny took three golliwogs, and as many other soft toys as she could squeeze in.

And then they were all ready. They were to go down by train, so Mummy and Daddy drove them to the big London station where their train waited for them. Cherry-Tree Farm was far away in the heart of the country, not very far from the sea. It would take them all day to get there.

"Good-bye, my dears!" said Mother. "Be good!"

"Good-bye!" said Daddy. "Remember that you will be in someone else's house, so do exactly as you are told, and help whenever you can!"

"Yes, we will!" shouted the children in excitement. "Good-bye, Mummy! Good-bye, Daddy! Have a good time in America! Don't forget to write to us!"

The engine whistled. Doors slammed. The guard waved a green flag and the train began to move slowly along the platform, chuffing as it went.

The chuffing grew faster. The platform came to an end. Mother and Daddy were only black specks in the distance, and the train came out of the big dark station into brilliant golden sunshine.

"We're off to Cherry-Tree Farm!" cried Rory, and he banged on the seat so that dust flew up in a cloud.

"We're going to go wild, we're going to go wild, we're going to go wild!" chanted Penny, in time to the noise that the train made. That made all the children laugh, and they sang Penny's funny little song for a long time. It was a good thing they were all alone in their carriage!

II

OFF TO CHERRY-TREE FARM

It was a very long journey, but most exciting. For one thing, Daddy had arranged that they should all have lunch in the dining-car, and it was quite exciting to walk down the rushing, rattling train and find their places at the little luncheon-tables. Rory had to hold on tightly to Penny, because she nearly fell over when the train swayed about.

The knives and forks rattled on the table, and Penny's bread jumped off its plate. Rory's water spilt on the table-cloth, but it wasn't his fault. It was funny to eat inside a train that was going at seventy miles an hour.

"If the train keeps up this speed it will soon be at Cherry-Tree Farm, I should think," said Penny, looking at the hedges and telegraph poles rushing by in a long line.

"We don't get there till after tea," said Sheila. "We've got to wait for tea till we're there, Mummy said. She said Auntie Bess would be sure to have it ready for us, and it would be a pity to spoil it by having tea on the train. So I guess we'd better eat as much dinner as we can, in case we get hungry."

They ate such an enormous meal that they all felt very sleepy afterwards. They staggered back along the rushing train, and found their carriage. Rory had promised his mother that he would make seven-year-old Penelope lie down after the midday meal, so he made a kind of bed for her on one seat.

"Come on, Penny," he said. "Here's a bed for you! Look, I've put my coat for a pillow, and I'll cover you up with this rug."

"But I want to be big like you, and talk," said Penny, who hated to be treated like a baby. But Rory was firm, and she had to lie down. In two minutes she was fast asleep.

And so was Rory! He leaned his head against the window, and although the train whistled and roared, he heard nothing of it — he was as fast asleep as little Penny.

It wasn't long before Sheila curled herself up like a kitten in her corner, and shut her eyes too. It was delicious to sleep in the swaying carriage. The noise it made crept into her dreams and made a song there — "We're going to go wild, we're going to go wild!"

Benjy stayed awake for a little while, thinking joyfully of the lovely holiday they were all going to have. Of the four children he was the one who most loved the country, and who longed most for the feel of animals and the song of the birds. The children had never been allowed to keep pets in London, so all that Benjy had been able to do was to make friends with the dogs in the park, and to feed the ducks there.

"Perhaps I shall have a puppy of my own," thought Benjy dreamily. "Perhaps there will be calves at the farm that will suck my hand — and maybe I shall find a badger's hole — or a fox's den."

And then he was fast asleep, and found himself sitting outside a fox's hole with his arm round a most peculiar yellow fox, who was smoking a pipe and saying that he wanted to go to America! Yes, Benjy was certainly asleep!

So, what with talking and having lunch and sleeping, it didn't really seem very long before the train drew up at a smally breezy station, and the porter there cried "Cherry-Woods, Cherry-Woods! Anyone for Cherry-Woods!"

"That's our station!" yelled Rory, in delight. "Come on, get your hats! Here's your bag, Sheila. Come on, Penny!

13

Hie, porter, there is some luggage of ours in the van!"

"It's coming out now, sir!" said the porter. And sure enough it was. Then Rory caught sight of Auntie Bess hurrying on to the platform, the wind blowing her dark hair into tight curls.

"Auntie Bess! Here we are!" yelled the four children, and they rushed to meet her.

"We had dinner on the train!" shouted Penny.

"Where's Uncle Tim?" asked Sheila, who loved her big, burly country uncle.

"Waiting outside with the trap," said Auntie Bess, kissing them. "My goodness, what pale cheeks! And what sticks of legs Benjy has got! I wonder you can walk on them, Benjy!"

Benjy went red. He hated his thin legs. He made up his mind to eat so much that his legs would be as fat as Uncle Tim's! And there *was* Uncle Tim, outside in the trap, waving his whip to the children.

What a noise there was as the four children clambered up into the pony-trap! Their luggage was coming along later in a farm-cart. The fat little brown pony turned round and looked at the children. She neighed joyfully.

"Why, even Polly, the pony, is pleased to see you!" laughed Uncle Tim. "Hallo, Penny! You've grown since I saw you!"

"Yes, I have," said Penny proudly. "I don't have a nurse now. I'm as grown-up as the others."

It was a very happy party that drove along the pretty country lanes to Cherry-Tree Farm. Here and there a tiny splash of green showed, where early honeysuckle leaves were out. Golden coltsfoot flowers gleamed on banks in the evening sunshine, and Penny and Benjy saw a sandy rabbit rushing away over a field, his white bobtail

flickering in the sunlight.

"I'm so hungry," said Rory, with a sigh. "I ate an enormous dinner, but I'm hungry again."

"Well, there's high tea waiting for you," said Auntie Bess. "Cold ham, and apple-pie and cheese, and buttery scones, and my own strawberry jam and those ginger buns you loved last time you came, and . . ."

"Oh, don't tell us any more, it makes me feel I can't wait," begged Penny.

But she had to wait until Polly, the pony, had trotted three miles to Cherry-Tree Farm. And there it was at last, shining in the last rays of the February sun, a rambling old farmhouse with a snug roof of brown thatch coming down so low in places that it touched Uncle Tim's hat.

The children washed and sat down to their meal. They ate and ate and ate. Benjy looked down at his legs to see if they had got any fatter — he felt as if they really must have grown already! Then up to bed they all went, much to their disappointment.

"Your mother said so," said Auntie Bess firmly. "You can go later to-morrow, but to-night you are tired with a very long journey. This is your bedroom, Sheila and Penny, and this one, opening off nearby, is the boys' room."

The two bedrooms were snuggled under the thatch, and had big brown beams running across the ceiling and through the walls. The floors were uneven, and the windows were criss-crossed with little panes.

"I do like a ceiling I can bump my head on in the corners," said Penny.

"Well, don't bump your head too often or you won't be quite so fond of my ceiling," said Auntie Bess. "Now hurry up and get into bed, all of you. Breakfast is at a quarter to eight. The bathroom is across the passage — you remember where it is, don't you? You can have either hot or cold baths in the morning — but please leave the bath clean and the bathroom tidy, or I shall come roaring at you like an angry bull!"

The children laughed. "We're going to go wild, you know, Auntie Bess!" called Penny.

"Not in the house, Penny, my dear, not in the house!" called back Auntie Bess, and she went downstairs, laughing.

"I'm so happy!" sang Benjy, as he slipped off his boots. "No more London! No more noise of buses and trams! No more poor sooty old trees! But clean sweet bushes and woods, bright flowers, singing birds and little shy animals slipping by. Oh, what fun!"

III

THE FIRST DAY AT THE FARM

Early next morning the sun slipped into the children's bedrooms and lay slanting across the walls. It was glorious to wake up in strange bedrooms, and to hear the hens clucking outside, and ducks quacking on the pond in the distance.

It didn't take the children long to bath and dress. Then down they went as the breakfast bell rang, and took their places at the white-clothed table.

Uncle Tim had been up for two hours, and came to breakfast as hungry as a hunter. "Hallo, sleepyheads!" he said. "I've been up and about for ages! A fine morning it is, too, though it was pitch-black when I slipped out of the farm door."

"Uncle, have you any calves?" asked Penny.

"Yes, two," said Uncle Tim. "You can see them after breakfast. And there are little lambs in the long meadow, and a foal in the field."

The children hurried through their breakfast and then went out to see everything. Sheila loved the little long-legged foal that shied away from her timidly when she held out her hand to it.

Benjy loved the two calves. He put his hand into the mouth of the little white one and it sucked it gently and lovingly. The brown calf butted its head against him and looked at him with soft brown eyes.

Then Shadow, the collie dog, came running up to him and rubbed against his legs. All dogs loved Benjy, and all cats, too! As soon as Shadow had gone to answer Uncle

Tim's whistle, three cats slipped out of the dark corners of the barn and mewed to Benjy.

"What a collection of cats!" said Benjy in his soft voice, and he scratched their heads.

Sheila and Penny had gone to see the lambs. There were thirty-three of them in the long meadow with their mother sheep. How they frisked and jumped! How they wriggled their long tails and maa-ed in their tiny high voices.

"Penny! Sheila!" suddenly called their aunt's voice. The two girls turned and saw Auntie Bess waving to them. "Will you do something for me?"

"Yes, of course!" shouted the girls, and they ran to see what it was that their aunt needed.

"You will find three little lambs by themselves in that pen over there," said Auntie Bess. "They have no mother, so I feed them from a milk-bottle. Would you like to feed them for me?"

"Oh *yes!*" cried the children, and they took the feeding-bottles that Auntie Bess held out to them.

"They are just like babies' bottles," said Sheila. "Do they really suck from these?"

"Yes," said Auntie Bess. "Come back to me for more milk when they have finished. They will need more than I have given you."

Penny and Sheila climbed through the fence and three tiny lambs came frisking up. When they saw the milk-bottles they were most excited. The biggest lamb of all put his front feet up on to Penny and tried to get at the bottle at once.

"Well, I'll feed you first," said Penny. "Oh, Sheila, do feed that tiny one. He looks so hungry."

But the tiny one didn't get a chance at first, for his brother pushed him away, took the teat of the bottle firmly

18

into his mouth and sucked away so hard that in a minute
or two the bottle was quite empty! Then Sheila ran back
for more milk and fed the tiny lamb. He was gentle and
sweet, and Sheila had to keep pushing his big brother
away. The girls gave the lambs two bottles each and then
went to wash them out ready for the next meal.

"I'd like to feed the lambs always, Auntie Bess," said
Penny. "And the chicks too – and the ducklings. Oh, do
look at those tiny ducks! Can I pick one up?"

"So long as you don't drop it and hurt it," said Auntie
Bess, going indoors. Penny picked up a bright yellow
duckling. It crept under her coat and huddled there. Penny
wished she could keep it there all day and night. It felt so
soft and warm.

That first day was a very happy one. It seemed so long,
and so full of sunshine. The children made friends with
all the animals except Bellow, the bull, who was kept in
a strong fenced paddock.

"He doesn't like strangers," said Uncle Tim. "Wait
till he is used to you before you go and sit on his fence and
talk to him. If you like you can go with Taffy when he
walks him every day."

Taffy was one of the farm-men. He took the big bull for
a short walk every day up the lane and down. Bellow had
a ring through his nose, and Taffy had a hooked stick
through his ring. He led the bull by this, and Bellow
stepped proudly up the lane and down, his red eyes
gleaming round at the watching children.

"I'd like to lead the bull for you one day, Taffy!" called
Rory, dancing up.

"I reckon it would be the bull that led *you*, Master
Rory!" said Taffy, with a grin. "Now don't you go dancing
round Bellow like that. He doesn't like it."

So Rory and the others went off to see the cows milked, and Bill and Ned, the two cowmen, let the children try their hands at milking.

Benjy was the best, for his hands were both strong and gentle. It was lovely to hear the creamy milk swishing into the pail. Penny was afraid of the cows at first, so she wouldn't try.

"You don't need to be afraid of Blossom and Daisy and Clover," said Ned, patting the cows' big sides.

Daisy looked round at Penny, and swished her tail gently. It hit the little girl and made her jump.

"She smacked me with her tail," said Penny indignantly. Everybody laughed.

"Well, you smack old Daisy with your hand and she'll be pleased enough!" grinned Ned, who was milking the big gentle cow.

When bedtime came at last the four children were more tired than they had been the day before. Penny could hardly undress herself and Sheila had to help her.

"My legs won't hold me up any more!" said Penny, and she fell on to her little white bed.

The others stayed up a little while, talking to their aunt and uncle round the lamp that gave a soft yellow light over the table. It was peaceful in the parlour. Shadow, the collie, lay at Uncle Tim's feet. A big white cat washed herself by the fire. Auntie Bess darned a stocking, and Uncle Tim listened to the children's chatter.

"Uncle, can we go for walks beyond the farm?" asked Benjy. "When I know all the animals on the farm I'd like to go and find some wild ones in the hills and woods."

"Yes. You can go where you like," said Uncle Tim. "But if Penny goes, you must take care of her, because she might fall into the river or ponds, or get lost by herself."

"Oh yes, we'll take care of Penny," promised Rory. "She can't always come with us, though, Uncle — because her legs are not as strong as ours are, and she couldn't walk as far as we do."

It was a good thing that Penny was in bed for she would not have been at all pleased to hear that! Although her legs were not so long as those of her brothers and sister she felt sure that they were just as good at walking and running. Poor Penny — she was always wishing that she wasn't so much smaller than the others! She didn't at all like being the baby of the family.

"Uncle, are there any badgers or otters about here?" asked Benjy, looking up from the book he was reading.

"There used to be badgers when I was a boy," said his uncle, lighting his old brown pipe and blowing out a cloud of blue smoke. "Those woods beyond the hill are called Brock Woods, you know, Benjy, and Brock is the old country name for badger."

"Perhaps there are still some there now," said Benjy, his eyes shining. "Is there anyone who could tell me, Uncle Tim?"

"I should think old Tammylan, the wild man, would know," said Uncle, and the children looked up in surprise.

"A *wild* man," said Sheila. "Are there wild men in this country then?"

"No, not really," said Uncle Tim. "We call him the wild man because he doesn't live in a house; he lives wild in the fields, and he looks queer — long hair and long beard, and funny clothes, you know. But people say that what he doesn't know about the animals and birds around here isn't worth knowing."

"I *wish* I knew him," said Benjy longingly. "What did you say his name was, Uncle?"

"Tammylan, he's called," said Uncle Tim, blowing out another cloud of smoke. "But don't you go hunting him out now, or you'll get into trouble. Last year he caught two boys and threw them into the river, and the year before that he caught young Dick Thomas and shook him so hard that his head nearly fell off."

"Why did he do that?" said Rory in surprise.

"We never really knew," said Auntie Bess, joining in the talk. "But we did know that the three boys were real rascals and deserved all they got! Still, it would be better if you didn't go hunting out old Tammylan, my dears. I wouldn't like you to be thrown into the river — especially if you can't swim!"

Well, of course, all three of the listening children at once made up their minds that they *would* go and hunt out the queer wild man of the hills as soon as they possibly could. They wouldn't go too near him — oh no! They would just watch out for him, see where he lived, and what he did. That would be fun. But they wouldn't let themselves be caught.

"We'll go hunting for old Tammylan next week," said Rory to Benjy, as they went upstairs to bed that night. "We'll find out from Taffy or Bill or Ned where he lives — and we'll go and see what he's like. Fancy — a real wild man!"

IV

THE HUNT FOR THE WILD MAN

The next few days were full of farmyard adventures, and for a time the children forgot about the wild man. Rory was chased by Bellow, the bull, and nearly got into serious trouble. Benjy just pulled him over the fence in time!

Rory had sat on the fence to watch the bull, and somehow he had fallen over. Bellow had seen him and had come rushing up in a trice, making a noise like his name! Rory had scrambled up, and Benjy had helped him over the fence just as the bull tore up to it.

"That was a near squeak!" said Rory, pretending that he wasn't at all frightened. "I say, won't the girls tremble to hear about that!"

They did tremble—but unluckily Penny told Uncle Tim, and Uncle Tim was not at all pleased. He sent for Rory and gave him a good talking-to.

"Don't play the fool," he said. "That sort of thing isn't funny. I'm in charge of you, and if you go and hurt yourself, I'm to blame. You're thirteen years old and I thought you could be trusted."

"I can, Uncle," said Rory, very red. "I won't go near the bull field again."

Then Penny was chased by a goose and tried to squeeze through some barbed wire. She tore her coat and scratched her arms very badly. She rushed in to Auntie Bess, screaming and crying.

"Well, I don't know who is the bigger goose," said Auntie Bess, putting some ointment on to the scratches.

"The goose is a silly goose for chasing a harmless little girl, and *you* are a silly goose for being frightened and running away. If you had said 'BO' to the goose, it would have gone off at once. Surely you are not one of those people who can't say 'bo' to a goose?"

"I *could* say 'bo'," said Penny at once, "but I just didn't think of it. I'll go right away now and practise saying 'bo' to that big grey goose over there."

All the same, she went to find Rory to take her, and how he laughed to hear Penny saying "Bo" as loudly as she could to a most alarmed goose, clinging on to his hand tightly all the time. The goose waddled away, cackling in fright, and Penny was simply delighted.

Sheila found a hen's nest out in the hedge, full of brown eggs. She was most surprised, and ran to tell her aunt.

Auntie Bess was pleased. "That's my naughty little hen, Brownie," she said. "I knew she was laying away, but I didn't know where. Bring in the eggs for me, Sheila. If Brownie wants to sit she shall, and we will have some more chicks then."

Benjy didn't get into any trouble. He was a quiet, dreamy boy, and he followed the farm-men about and watched them, fed the animals and birds, went walking across the farm with his uncle, and wished he was old enough to smoke an old brown pipe. Uncle Tim looked so contented and comfortable as he leaned on a gate, looking at his wide fields, with his pipe in his mouth. Benjy leaned too, and pretended that he was puffing away at a pipe, though his pipe was only a bit of twig.

After the excitement of the first few days had worn off the three older children began to think about Tammylan again.

"I saw a little spire of blue smoke this evening, away on

24

the hill over there," said Rory, waving his hand to the distant woods. "I think it must have been Tammylan cooking his supper."

"Who's Tammylan?" asked Penny at once.

"A wild man," said Sheila.

"Fibber!" said Penny.

"No, really, it's true, Penny," said Benjy, and he told her what Uncle Tim had said about Tammylan. "And we are going to find him one day and see what he's like!" said Benjy.

"Oh!" said Penny, in excitement. "Can I come too?"

"I don't think so," said Rory. "You see, it might be a long way. And Tammylan might be very wild and frighten you."

"I don't care how far away it is, and I know I wouldn't be frightened!" said Penny obstinately. "I'm coming. You're not to leave me out."

"Well, we'll see, Penny," said Rory. Penny sulked. She knew what "We'll see," meant. It meant "You won't come." But she was quite determined to go, and she made up her mind that she would not let the others out of her sight at all. Wherever they went, she would go.

"I may be only seven, but I'll just show them I'm not a baby!" thought Penny fiercely. "I'm as strong as Rory, and he's thirteen. I *won't* be left out!"

So for the next day or two the little girl followed the others about everywhere till they got quite tired of her.

"Can't you go and find something to do on your own?" said Sheila at last. "You just come tagging after us all the time, and you'll get so tired."

But Penny wouldn't go off on her own. So when the others did decide to go and look for Tammylan they had to talk about it when Penny was in bed.

Sheila went to sit on the boys' big white bed, whilst Penny was lying asleep in the other room. They talked in whispers.

"We'll get Auntie Bess to give us sandwiches to take for our lunch," whispered Sheila. "We'll go off for a picnic. We'll make for Brock Woods. Taffy told me to-day that Tammylan is most often seen there."

"Good!" said Rory, hugging his knees. "But what about Penny?"

"We can't take her," said Benjy. "She's too little. I know, Sheila—you can tell her she may feed all the lambs to-morrow morning by herself. She will be so pleased—and whilst she is doing it we'll slip off."

"Well, I hope she won't mind too much," said Sheila. "She does so hate being left out of things because she's younger—but we can't make her older, however much we want to!"

Well, the next day Rory begged Auntie Bess to give them a picnic lunch, and she nodded her head at once.

"It's a fine sunny March day," she said, "and if you promise not to sit on the damp grass, I'll let you have a picnic. But what about Penny?"

"She'd better stay behind with you, Aunt Bess," said Sheila. "She really isn't big enough to walk for miles."

"Well, I'll make it up to her somehow," said Auntie Bess. "Come for your sandwiches in half an hour and they will be ready."

So in half an hour the three children went to fetch their picnic lunch. Auntie Bess had put it into two bags. One had the eatables, and the other carried two big bottles of creamy milk.

Penny was feeding the three lambs, happy because she was doing it all by herself. Rory, Sheila, and Benjy slipped off with their lunch and made their way down the sunken lane towards the far-off woods. The March sun shone down and warmed them. The celandines in the lane lifted up their polished faces and smiled. It was a lovely day for an adventure.

"I wonder if we'll find Tammylan!" said Sheila, skipping along. "I wonder what he'll be like. I'd love to see a wild man."

"Sheila, if you're going to skip like that you'd better give *me* the milk," said Benjy. "You'll turn it all into butter before we get to the woods!"

So Benjy carried the milk and Sheila skipped like a month-old lamb, whilst Rory plodded along with a crook-stick that Uncle Tim had given him.

"It's fun to be in the country like this!" said Sheila. "Fancy—all we'd see in town now would be a few trees and a bit of grass, unless we went to the parks. And out here we're going to look for a wild man!"

They came to the end of the lane and climbed over a stile. They went across the field and over another stile. Then the path led into Brock Woods. It was dark under the evergreen trees, but when they came to where oak and hazel grew the woods were lighter.

A farm-boy came along whistling, Rory stopped him. "I say!" said Rory. "Do you know where Tammylan lives?"

"No, I don't, and I don't want to, either," said the farm-lad. "You let him be. He's wild, he is."

"Oh, but do tell us whereabouts he lives," begged Benjy. "We just want to see him, that's all."

"He's much more likely to see you than you are to see *him*," said the boy. "Well, I don't rightly know all his hiding-places, but folk do say he has a cave or two in the hill yonder."

"Oh, thank you!" said the children and went on their way through the wood. They came to the steep hill at last, covered with heather, birch trees, gorse, and bracken.

"Now we must be quiet and look for the caves," whispered Rory. "Come on!"

The children went in single file round the hill, looking for caves. But to their surprise, no matter how carefully they looked, they could find no cave at all. Not one.

"Well," said Rory, after about half an hour, "I don't believe there's a cave larger than a rabbit's burrow anywhere in this hill! That farm-lad was telling stories."

"Let's sit down and have our lunch," said Sheila. "I'm so hungry I could eat the paper round the sandwiches!"

"All right," said Benjy. "You eat that, and we'll have the sandwiches, Sheila!"

Auntie Bess had made them a lovely picnic lunch. There were ham sandwiches, hard-boiled eggs in their shells, each with a screw of salt beside them, slices of sticky gingerbread, last autumn's yellow apples, and half a bottle of milk each.

"I wonder why food tastes so much nicer out of doors than indoors," said Rory, munching hard. The children had spread out Rory's mackintosh and were sitting on it, leaning back against a big old oak tree, with the March sun shining warmly down through the bare branches.

"What shall we do after our lunch?" asked Sheila. "Shall we look for Tammylan again?"

"Yes," said Benjy. "And we'll pick some primroses and violets for Aunt Bess. And if I can find some frog spawn I'd like to take it home and put it into a jar. I've never seen tadpoles turn into frogs."

"How are you going to take the frog spawn home?" asked Rory.

"In my hands," said Benjy.

"You *are* silly!" cried Sheila. "It's like a lump of jelly. You'll never be able to carry slippery jelly all the way home."

"Well, I'll have a jolly good try," said Benjy. "Come on, you others. Haven't you finished yet?"

"Yes, but I wish I hadn't," said Sheila, with a sigh. "That was a gorgeous meal."

They all got up and brushed the crumbs from themselves. The empty milk-bottles went back into the bag. The paper off the sandwiches and cake blew away through the trees. Not one of the children thought of picking it up

and taking it home again, so that the woods might be clean and tidy.

They set off to look for a pond, keeping a sharp look out for the wild man all the time. But they didn't see a sign of him — though, if they had looked very carefully indeed, they would have seen a pair of sharp brown eyes peering at *them* every now and again through the bushes.

After a long time they came to a pond. There was a little moor-hen on it, swimming fast, her head bobbing to and fro like clockwork. The children laughed to see her.

"Any frog spawn here?" said Benjy. He stooped down to look. He could see the blunt noses of the frogs poking up here and there — and then, in a far corner, he saw a floating mass of jelly — the frog spawn.

Benjy ran round to the other side of the pond. He balanced carefully on an old log and crept out to where he saw the frog spawn. He bent down to pick it up in his hands.

He lifted a big patch of it. It slipped from his hands and went flop into the water! He tried again — but no sooner did he get hold of it than it seemed to wriggle out of his hands like a live thing. Rory and Sheila shouted with laughter at him.

"Try again, Benjy!" they laughed. "Try again!"

Benjy tried and tried, but it wasn't a bit of good. At last he grabbed a piece in both hands and held it tightly against his coat to keep it from slipping — and just at that very moment a startling thing happened.

There came a scream, loud and frightened, not very far off — and the scream was Penny's! All the children knew it at once, and they looked at one another, alarmed and surprised.

Benjy tried to jump back from his log — his foot slipped,

and into the pond he went, flat on his face! He floundered there for a moment and then came up, gasping and spluttering. Rory rushed round to help him out.

"You idiot, Benjy!" he said. "Just look at your coat! You *will* get into a row!"

"Quick! Help me up! Was that Penny we heard?" gasped Benjy, spitting out bits of frog spawn from his mouth. "Don't bother about *me*. What's the matter with Penny?"

All three children rushed in the direction of the scream. And then, far away, they saw somebody carrying Penny, and on the breeze they could hear the sound of crying.

"It's Penny all right! She came to look for us, I expect — and oh, do you think Tammylan has got her?"

"Quick! Quick! We must rescue her!" shouted Rory. And off they ran at top speed to find poor Penny.

V

PENNY HAS AN ADVENTURE BY HERSELF

When Penny had been left alone at the farm feeding the three lambs, she had felt very happy. It was the first time she had fed them all by herself and she was pleased.

But when she had finished, and had washed the milk-bottles well, she began to look for the others. Then she was *not* so pleased.

"Rory!" she shouted. "Where are you? Sheila! Benjy! Oh, do come and play with me!"

Auntie Bess came out of the farmhouse and called to Penny.

"They're gone for a very long walk, darling. It was too far for you to go. I want you to come and help me make some tarts this morning. Would you like that?"

"No, thank you," said Penny, almost in tears. "I do think it's mean of the others to go off without me. My legs are quite as strong as theirs."

Nothing that her aunt could say would make Penny any happier, so in the end Aunt Bess gave it up. "Well, just play round the farmyard and have some fun," she said, and went indoors to her baking.

Angry and hurt, Penny wandered round the farmyard for a while. But she didn't feel like playing with anything. Shadow, the collie, came up and licked her hand but she pushed him away. Snowy, the big white cat, came and rubbed against her legs, but that didn't please cross little Penny either.

And then she made up her mind to go and find the

others! Yes—she would go all by herself and just show them that she could walk as far as they could!

"I guess I know where they've gone!" said Penny. "They've gone to find Tammylan, the wild man! They think he lives over in Brock Woods there, away by the hill. That's where they've gone. Well, I'll go too! I'll just show them how I can walk."

The little girl said nothing to her aunt. She slipped away through the gate, out into the lane and ran down it as fast as she could. She began to puff and pant after a while, and she slowed down. She sat for a moment on the stile, then jumped down and began to run again.

"I hope I don't meet the wild man," she thought to herself. "I don't think I'd like that. Now, is this the path to the woods?"

It was. Penny ran down it, and after a long while she came to the hill which the children had searched for caves some time back. They had had their lunch and had gone to find frog spawn. But Penny knew they had been there.

"There's the paper wrapping from their sandwiches!" said the little girl to herself. "Oh dear—it does make me feel hungry to think of sandwiches. I wish I'd got something to eat. I wonder if they've got any left."

Penny didn't know what to do next. She had no idea where the others had gone. She was hungry and tired—and lost! She didn't know the path home. She only knew she was very tired and miserable. She wished she hadn't gone to look for the others now.

"I know what I'll do," said Penny, trying to be brave. "I'll climb up a tree! Then maybe I shall see where the others are—or perhaps I shall see Cherry-Tree Farm, and then I can make my way home."

Penny was not used to climbing trees. There were very

few to climb in London. But she ran to a tree that looked easy to climb and did her best to get as high as she could.

But Penny did not know the right way to climb trees. She didn't know how to test each branch before she set her weight on it, to make sure that it would bear her. And suddenly, when she was half-way up the tree, the branch she was standing on broke beneath her!

Penny clutched the branch above her in fright. She was standing on nothing! She screamed long and loudly — and that was the scream that the others heard.

"Oh help, help!" wept poor Penny. "I shall fall. My arms won't keep me up any longer!"

And then a voice below her spoke clearly. "Let yourself fall, little girl. I will catch you. You will be quite safe."

Penny tried to look down, but she couldn't. She didn't dare to let herself fall — but she had to, because her arms gave way, and down she went.

Yes, down she went — but not to fall on the hard ground and perhaps break her leg. No — she fell straight into two strong arms that were ready for her! Somebody caught her, somebody held her, and somebody comforted her.

Penny looked up through her tears. She saw a dark-brown face out of which looked two brown eyes with queer yellow flecks in them. A curly brown and grey beard grew from the chin, and the man's hair was rather long, and curly too.

"You're quite safe!" said her rescuer. "I caught you beautifully, didn't I! Don't cry any more."

"My arm hurts," said Penny, sobbing. She had scraped her arm on a sharp twig as she fell, and it had made a deep cut. Her arm was bleeding under her torn coat.

The man who had caught her set her on the ground and looked at her arm. "A nasty cut," he said. "We'll soon put

34

that right, though. Come along with me."

But Penny was so tired and hungry and had had such a shock that her legs wouldn't walk. So her friend had to carry her in his arms, down the hill through the bracken and heather. Penny sobbed as they went, and felt very sorry for herself indeed.

"Why did you come out all alone, so far from home?" asked the man. "You shouldn't do that."

"The others went off by themselves to look for Tammylan, the wild man," said Penny, rubbing the tears from her cheeks.

"Why did they want to look for him?" asked her friend.

"Oh, they thought it would be fun to see a real wild man," said Penny. "But I would be afraid if I met him."

"No, you wouldn't," said her friend.

"Yes, I would," said Penny. "I would run and run and run!"

"And instead of running and running, do you know what you did? You jumped right into my arms!" said the man, with a laugh.

Penny looked up at his face in surprise. "What do you mean?" she said. "*You're* not Tammylan, are you?"

"Yes, I am," said Tammylan. "I don't know why people call me the wild man. All I do is to live by myself in the woods and hills, and learn the ways of my little furred and feathered friends. Well, little girl—are you afraid of the wild man?"

"No!" said Penny, beginning to feel really excited. "Oh, Tammylan—I've found you, and the others haven't! Aren't I lucky?"

"I don't know about that," said Tammylan. "Now—can you stand down for a minute. Here we are, at one of my little hidey-holes!"

Penny stood and looked. Tammylan was moving a curtain of bracken away from a hole in the hillside. Behind it a cave showed its dark mouth — a cave with heather dropping down from the top edge, and close-growing plants trimming the sides. It looked exciting.

"I want to see inside," said Penny. "And oh, Tammylan, have you got anything I could eat? It does seem such a long time since my breakfast!"

"I have some soup made from all kinds of queer roots," said Tammylan in his clear, low voice. "I will make it warm for you."

Penny bent down and went inside the cave. It opened out widely inside, and the ceiling became high. A rocky ledge ran along one side and on it was a rough bed of dried bracken and heather. On a rocky shelf were a few tin plates and other things.

At first Penny could see nothing inside, but as soon as her eyes grew used to the half-darkness she could see everything clearly. She liked it. It was really exciting. She was in the cave of the wild man!

"Wouldn't my brothers and my sister be jealous if they could see me here!" said Penny. "Oh dear — my arm does hurt me, Tammylan!"

"I'm just getting some water to bathe it with and some of my special ointment to put on the cut," said Tammylan from the back of the cave. "I believe I saw your brothers and sister this morning."

"Oh, I wonder where they are now," said Penny. "I'd really like them to share this adventure with me, although they did leave me out of their walk!"

Rory, Sheila, and Benjy were not very far away! They had tracked the wild man and Penny almost up to the cave. Now they were whispering together behind a bush to decide how to rescue their little sister.

"We'll all make a rush, and we'll shout and yell like Red Indians!" said Rory. "Then, in the excitement, we'll grab Penny and run off with her. Now, are you ready?"

"Yes," said Sheila and Benjy. They ran to the mouth of the cave, shouting and yelling, and forced their way inside, looking for Penny.

But it was so dark that at first they could see nothing. They stood there, blinking—and then they heard Penny's voice.

"Oh Rory! Oh Sheila—and Benjy! You did make me jump. How did you find me? Oh Rory—what do you think? I've found Tammylan, the wild man!"

"Where is he?" asked Rory, his eyes getting used to the dark cave. "We thought he had caught you, Penny. We heard you scream, and we came to rescue you."

"I screamed because I was climbing a tree and the branch broke," said Penny. "Tammylan held out his arms and I fell into them. Then he carried me here to see to my cut arm. I caught it on a twig."

The three children began to feel rather silly. A deep voice came from the other end of the cave. "Please sit down for a moment. I am glad you wanted to rescue your sister—but she really isn't in any danger at present!"

The three children sat down on the heather bed. So Penny had found the wild man, and they hadn't! They were simply longing to ask dozens of questions, but there was something in Tammylan's voice that stopped them. They suddenly felt that they must be on their best behaviour. It was queer.

So there they all sat, waiting for the wild man they had wanted so much to find.

VI

TAMMYLAN AND HIS CAVE

Tammylan came out of the darkness holding a small bowl of water. Penny was surprised.

"Have you got a tap at the back of the cave, Tammylan?" she asked. Tammylan laughed.

"No," he said. "But a little spring comes from a hole in the rock there, and then runs down through the floor of the cave. It is very cold and clear, and I use it for my drinking-water. Now, where's that arm?"

Penny slipped off her coat, which was badly torn. Tammylan bathed her arm gently and then put some queer-smelling yellow ointment on it. Penny sniffed at it.

"What is it?" she asked. "I like the smell."

"Oh, it's made of all kinds of herbs and roots," said Tammylan. "You wouldn't know any of them. It will heal your cut more quickly than anything out of a chemist's shop."

"It feels nice," said Penny. Tammylan took her handkerchief and bound up her arm neatly. Penny looked up at Rory.

"I suppose you haven't any sandwiches left?" she asked. "I haven't had any dinner and I'm so hungry."

"Not one," said Rory. "I'd have saved you some if I'd known, Penny."

"You shall soon have some food," said Tammylan, and he lit a little fire at the doorway of his cave, on a flat stone that had been often used before. He cooked some broth in a pot, stirring it with a twig. It smelt simply delicious.

The others gazed enviously at Penny when the soup was ready and she was eating it. It made them feel hungry even to smell it. Penny said it was the nicest soup she had ever had in her life.

Tammylan suddenly saw that Benjy was wet and was shivering. He felt the boy's coat.

"So you fell into the pond where you were looking for frog spawn!" he said. "Go to the back of the cave and take off your wet things. You will find an old rug there. Wrap yourself in it and come back to the fire. I will dry your things for you. You can't go home like that."

Very soon Benjy was sitting by a roaring fire, wearing an old red rug. He said he only wanted a few feathers in his hair to feel like a real Red Indian.

"You live a sort of Red Indian life, don't you, Tammylan?" he asked. "Do you know, we heard all sorts of dreadful stories about you."

"Did you?" said Tammylan, as if he was not at all interested.

"Yes," said Rory. "We heard that you had shaken a boy called Dick Thomas till his head nearly flew off!"

"That was quite true," said Tammylan. The children stared at him in surprise. Tammylan seemed so gentle and kind.

Tammylan spoke sternly. "Dick Thomas found a bird with a broken wing," he said. "And the poor thing couldn't get away from him — so he tormented it. I won't tell you how, but he was very cruel. That is why I shook him as I did."

"Oh," said Rory. He thought for a moment and then asked Tammylan another question. "Why did you throw two boys into the river?"

"Dear me, so you heard that too, did you?" said

Tammylan. "Well, they had a dog they didn't want — so they tied a brick to him and threw him into the river to drown. I came by, took out the dog — and threw the boys in. That's all."

"Could they swim?" asked Benjy.

"Of course," said Tammylan. "I didn't tie bricks to them! Don't you think they deserved a ducking?"

"Oh *yes*," said Rory. "I do."

There was a pause — and suddenly Tammylan lifted up his hand to stop everyone from speaking. He had heard a small sound that had escaped everyone else's ears.

The children sat still and looked towards the cave entrance. They saw a pair of big ears — then a pair of large, anxious eyes — and then a brown rabbit slipped round the fire and came into the cave. When it saw the children it stopped in fear. It sat up on its hind legs, its nose sniffing and woffling, and its whiskers trembling.

"Well, Bobtail," Tammylan said in his deep, clear voice. "Have you come to pay me your usual visit? Don't be afraid of the children."

The rabbit came a little nearer, sniffed at Tammylan's outstretched hand, and then, frightened at a sudden movement made by Sheila, he turned and fled, his white bobtail showing as he went.

"Oh!" said Benjy, too delighted for words. "Tammylan! Is he a tame rabbit?"

"No," said Tammylan. "He is a wild one. One night he got into a trap, and his leg was broken. He squealed pitifully, and I went to free him. I set his leg and it healed. Now he is one of my friends and comes to see me every day."

"*One* of your friends?" asked Benjy at once. "How do you mean? Are other animals your friends too?"

"Oh yes," said Tammylan. "Birds as well. They all come to me. They show me their homes and their little ones. I share their lives. I am as wild as they are, you see!"

"Tammylan, please, Tammylan, will you show me your friends?" begged Benjy, taking Tammylan's brown freckled hand, that seemed more like a paw, it was so thin and brown. "I've read books about birds and animals for years, but I've always lived in London till now. I'll never get a chance like this again—so will you please, please let me know your friends!"

"And me too?" asked Penny.

"Do you want to make friends with badgers and foxes, with toads and frogs, otters and wild birds?" asked Tammylan. "No! You children don't care for any of those things nowadays! You want toys of all kinds—cinemas—bicycles to ride—roller skates. Oh, *I* know! All you want of animals is to tease them and frighten them—to take their eggs, to throw stones at them. No—my friends are my own, and I share them with nobody."

"Oh, Tammylan, you are wrong!" cried Sheila. "Children aren't all like that. Just because you've seen a few that were cruel and stupid doesn't mean that we are all like that. Can't you give us a chance and see? Anyway, give Benjy a chance. Benjy has been mad on animals and birds all his life but he's never even had a dog to call his own."

Tammylan didn't say anything for a minute, and his eyes looked far away.

"Even Benjy cared so little for my woods this morning that he let the wind blow away your papers," he said at last. "They will go pulpy with the rain. They will wrap themselves around my primroses and violets, and will make my woods look ugly and untidy."

The children went red. They remembered that Auntie Bess had told them not to litter the countryside with paper or bottles.

"We shouldn't have done that," said Benjy. "I'm sorry, Tammylan. We'll look for the papers on our way home and pick them up. We'll never spoil the country again like that."

"I have picked up your papers already," said Tammylan. "You didn't see me, but I was there."

The children all felt ashamed — except Penny, who had had no papers to throw away. But she was ashamed for the others.

"Benjy may come and see me again," said Tammylan at last. "He has the low voice and the quiet hands of those who love the wild creatures, Benjy may come — and maybe, if my friends like him, I will let you others come sometimes too."

"Oh, thank you!" cried Benjy, his face shining. "I'll come! I won't make a single noise or movement if you'll let me see the friends that come to visit you. I'll tell the others all about it, and then maybe you'll let them come too, another time."

"I won't make any promises," said Tammylan. "Now, Benjy, your clothes are dry and I am sure it must be long past your teatime. Get into them and go home. Come again after tea the day after to-morrow — by yourself."

Benjy was overjoyed. He got quickly into his almost-dry clothes. Then they all said good-bye to Tammylan, and left his exciting cave, talking nineteen to the dozen.

"Well, that *was* an adventure!" said Benjy. "Fancy the wild man turning out to be such a grand person. Before you know it, I'm going to be friends with all the otters and badgers and hares and rabbits in the countryside!"

"Don't be so sure," said Rory, half-jealous. "Tammylan won't stand any nonsense. You might get thrown into the river."

"I shan't," said Benjy, and he knew quite well he wouldn't. "I say — is that Uncle Tim coming to meet us?"

It was — he had come to find Penny, for when she had not gone in to her midday meal Auntie Bess had been very worried indeed. Now it was almost teatime.

Auntie Bess didn't want to hear about Tammylan — she wanted to know where Penny had been, and what she had been doing! Penny found herself being well scolded!

"Why didn't you come and tell me you were going?" scolded Auntie Bess.

"Because I knew you wouldn't let me," said Penny, beginning to cry. "Don't be cross with me. I climbed a tree and I fell down, and I cut my arm, and I didn't have any dinner. . . ."

"Well, that was your own fault," said Auntie Bess. "Now don't you do such a thing again. Come along in and have tea. You must be as hungry as hunters."

They were! There wasn't much left of the veal and ham pie, the jam tarts, and the cherry cake when the four children had finished!

"What an adventure we all had!" said Benjy that night when they went to bed. "I did enjoy it — and to think it's only just beginning! Aren't we lucky!"

"*You* are!" said Rory. "You're the one that's going to have the luck, it seems to me."

"Well, I'll do my best to share it with you," said Benjy sleepily. "I'll tell you everything."

Then off he went to sleep, to dream of a tame rabbit that came to clean his shoes and cook soup for him and dry his clothes!

VII

BENJY PAYS A VISIT

After tea two days later Benjy said good-bye to the others and slipped off to Tammylan's cave. He felt excited. What was he going to see?

As he came near to the cave he saw Tammylan sitting outside. Tammylan nodded to Benjy. "So you are none the worse for your soaking!" he said. "Come along in. I am expecting visitors this evening!"

Benjy was soon sitting on the bed of dry heather and bracken. "Don't talk," said Tammylan. "And don't move, no matter what you see!"

Benjy sat quite still. He even tried not to breathe, but he just *had* to do that. And suddenly someone appeared at the cave opening! Someone with large upright ears, big eyes and a furry coat.

"The rabbit!" whispered Benjy in delight.

"No. A hare," answered Tammylan, and he made a low animal-like noise. The hare scudded in and sat at Tammylan's feet, his whiskers quivering. Tammylan's lean brown fingers caressed the long ears, and the hare sat perfectly still, enjoying the quiet fondling. Benjy longed to put out his hand and touch the hare too, but he did not dare to. It might frighten it and make it leap away.

Tammylan began to speak to the listening animal. At first he said a lot of nonsense that Benjy couldn't understand—and then he slipped some sense into his talking, and Benjy listened because Tammylan was telling him all about the hare.

"You should know a hare from a rabbit, Benjy," said

Tammylan, still caressing the hare's long ears. "See these long, long ears with their black tips — and see how long the hare's hind legs are. Soon you will see a rabbit and you will notice the difference."

The hare stirred under Tammylan's fingers and the wild man ran his fingers down the animal's spine. "Now don't stir, little brown hare. I am only telling your story to this young friend of mine. Speak in a low voice to the hare, Benjy — maybe he will not be afraid of you, now that he is used to your smell."

Benjy spoke in his softest voice. "Little brown hare, don't be afraid of me. Where do you live?"

The hare started when Benjy spoke, but Tammylan's fingers went on stroking his ears and he sat back again, looking up at Benjy out of his enormous eyes.

"So you will be friends with Benjy, brown hare?" said Tammylan. "Shall we tell him where you live?"

"In a burrow, like the rabbits?" asked Benjy, longing to feel the hare's long ears.

"No, no," said Tammylan. "The hare is no lover of underground ways. He likes the fresh open air. He lives in the fields, in a hiding-place called a 'form' because it takes the shape or form of his body. Sometimes he makes his form among the thickets of briar and gorse—but this hare has his home in one of your uncle's fields. Ah, he is a clever fellow, this little brown hare. Many a time he has been chased by the sly red fox, and has thrown him off the scent."

"How does he do that, Tammylan?" asked Benjy.

"I have watched him," answered Tammylan. "If the red fox is after him, he will suddenly leap twelve or fifteen feet to the side, and break his track in that way. The fox finds that it comes to a sudden end—and by the time he has found the new track, my little brown hare is far, far away. When he leaves his form at dusk to go and feed, he plays the same trick—he leaps suddenly to one side, and so breaks the trail to his hiding-place."

"Clever little hare," said Benjy. "Oh, look, Tammylan—here are some more visitors!"

Some small creatures appeared at the mouth of the cave. Against the setting sun they seemed dark—but their long ears told the two watchers what they were.

"Rabbits this time," said Tammylan. "They always come at dusk. They do not mind the hare—but if the red fox is here, or the striped badger, they will not even come near the entrance."

"Oh, does the fox . . ." began Benjy, in surprise—and then he stopped. He had raised his voice, and the rabbits had fled. The hare too started in alarm and would have gone if Tammylan's hand had not restrained it.

"Sorry, Tammylan," said Benjy. "I forgot."

"Say no more for a while," said Tammylan. "I will sing my song and maybe they will come back."

Tammylan's song was queer. It wasn't really a song at all. It was the sound of the wind in the trees, the noise of a babbling brook, the rustle of leaves in the hedge—all the sounds that animals know and trust.

And soon the rabbits came back again, their long ears outlined against the fading light. "Come!" said Tammylan. "Come little friends! I am here!"

The rabbits scampered in. There were three of them. They came to Tammylan's feet, but they would not even touch Benjy. He was there with Tammylan, so he must be all right, but he was not yet their friend.

Tammylan lifted the smallest rabbit on to his knee. In the evening light that streamed into the cave Benjy could see its twitching, never-still nose, its long ears and wide eyes.

"You will see that this little rabbit's ears are not so long as the hare's," said Tammylan, and he stroked them. "Nor have they the black tips. Ah, little rabbit, you were not really made for an underground life, with these large ears, were you?"

"What does it do with its ears when it goes underground?" asked Benjy in wonder.

"It lays them flat over its back, like this," said Tammylan, and he placed the rabbit's ears down on its back. "Now, little rabbit, shall we go to see your home? Will you show us how you build it, with your strong forepaws?"

The animals seemed to understand what he said to

them. They ran to the entrance of the cave, sat upright there for a moment or two, and then scampered away, their white bobtails showing clearly as they ran.

"Where have they gone?" asked Benjy, disappointed.

"To their playground, outside their home," said Tammylan. "Come, we will follow them."

In a few minutes Tammylan and Benjy were sitting behind a big gorse bush. On the other side, clearly to be seen, were rabbits of all sizes — playing, feeding, running. Benjy felt as if he could watch them all night long!

The hare appeared beside them again, and watched the rabbits too. One rabbit sat up and began to wash itself, putting down first one ear and then the other to clean them thoroughly.

"See, Benjy," said Tammylan in a low voice, "there is a rabbit scraping a new hole in the hillside! See how he does it!"

Benjy watched. The rabbit scratched at the earth with its strong forepaws, and sent it flying behind it with its hindpaws.

"Is the hill full of rabbit-burrows?" whispered Benjy.

"Yes," said Tammylan. "If you were small enough to explore them you would have a fine time, Benjy! You could go from the top of the hill to the bottom by their underground passages. You would see that here and there they have been sensible enough to make the passages a bit wider — for passing-places."

"Oh, how I wish I could go inside and see," said Benjy. "Oh, listen, Tammylan — what is that rabbit doing?"

One of the big rabbits was drumming on the hillside with his back legs. At the sound, all the rabbits looked up in alarm. Then one by one they fled to the nearest burrow, their white scuts bobbing up and down behind them. The hare silently disappeared.

"Why have they gone?" asked Benjy. "Did I make a noise?"

"No. They have smelt the red fox!" said Tammylan, getting up. "He is about now. Come, it is time for you to go home to *your* burrow too, Benjy! I will take you part of the way—and you shall see the hare's form as we go."

The boy and the man went down the hill and into the dark wood. Tammylan moved as surely as a cat in the dark of the trees, but Benjy could hardly see. Tammylan had to take his arm and guide him.

They came to the open fields. Tammylan walked swiftly towards the middle of one. He made a curious noise, and the hare appeared silently beside them again.

"We have come to see your form, brown hare," said Tammylan. "Where is it? Are we near?"

The hare gave an enormous leap sideways and disappeared for a moment. Then Benjy saw his long ears a good way away.

"He has broken his trail, as I told you he does," said Tammylan. They went towards the hare, who led them a little way farther, and then they came upon his form—a cosy dent in the ground, well hidden from prying eyes.

The hare lay down in it to show Tammylan that it was his. Benjy thought he was a marvellous hare. "Has he got a wife?" he asked Tammylan. "Does she have a form, too?"

"Yes," said Tammylan. "And soon after they are born her little ones make their own tiny forms, and lie there hidden safely—as safe as the baby rabbits that are born underground. Now come, hare, let us see you run!"

The hare came with them over the field—and then, at a sign from Tammylan he ran in the dim light across the big field. Benjy could see his white bobtail.

"I know why we say 'as swift as a hare' now," said the boy. "I never saw anything run so fast before! Why do we say 'As mad as a March hare' sometimes, Tammylan? Are hares mad in March?"

"Quite mad!" said Tammylan. "They kick and buck, they box with one another, they leap and bound about in the most ridiculous way. Perhaps you will see them this month, Benjy. Now I will leave you here. Come and see me another day and meet some more of my friends. Bring little Penny. Good-night."

"Good-night," said Benjy. He stopped and watched Tammylan slip away in the dusk. He heard the wild man give a curious call, and the hare answered it. "Ohnt, ohnt!" said Tammylan, and the hare said the same. Then, with the hare at his heels, Tammylan disappeared over the evening fields, and Benjy, tired and happy, ran back to Cherry-Tree Farm, full of his queer adventure.

VIII

TAMMYLAN AND THE SNAKES

Penny, Rory and Sheila were never tired of hearing Benjy tell about his evening with Tammylan. They decided to tell their aunt and uncle all about it too.

Auntie Bess and Uncle Tim were astonished. "I'll go along and see this queer fellow," said Uncle Tim. "I'd better see if he's all right for you to go about with."

So he went along. The children were rather cross about it. "Suppose Uncle says we mustn't go with him!" said Benjy. "I really can't obey him! I do like Tammylan so much, and I mean to learn all he can teach me about his furred and feathered friends!"

"You can't disobey Uncle Tim," said Penny. "We are staying in his house. We *must* do what he says."

Luckily for the children Uncle Tim liked Tammylan. "He's a strange chap," he said to Auntie Bess. "Says he doesn't like the way men behave to one another, so he prefers to live with the animals. He says he can trust *them*. Well, well—his ideas about rabbits and foxes are not mine. He wouldn't want to make friends of those tiresome rabbits if they spoilt his crops as they spoil mine—and he wouldn't think the fox such a fine creature either, if it killed his chickens! Well, we don't all think alike, and it won't do the children any harm to learn a bit about the ways of our animals and birds. There's Penny here wanted to know if goats laid eggs the other day!"

Rory, Sheila, and Benjy screamed with laughter. Penny went red. "You shouldn't tell tales of me, Uncle," she said.

"No, I shouldn't," said Uncle Tim, patting her head. "Never mind! I could make you laugh at some of the things the other have said to me too. Now, let me see, who was it wanted to know where the turkeys' pond was?"

It was Sheila's turn to go red. Auntie Bess laughed. "Well, you can't expect town children to know much," she said. "If Tammylan can teach them something they will love it. You and I are too busy to take them about much."

"I've got to take Penny with me next time I go," said Benjy. "It's her turn. Can I take her, Aunt Bess?"

"Benjy will get more turns than anyone," grumbled Rory.

"Well, you'd better practise moving and speaking quietly," said Benjy. "You and Sheila are such noisy creatures. A rabbit would run a mile as soon as he heard you coming!"

"Benjy, when can we go to see Tammylan?" asked Penny eagerly. "Can we go to-day?"

"Not to-day!" said Auntie Bess. "It looks too much like rain. Wait for a really sunny day."

Two days later the sun shone down and felt as hot as in July. March had come in like a lion, and was going out like a lamb.

"It's the last day of March to-day," said Benjy. "We'll go and find Tammylan if you like, Penny. Let's go this morning."

So off they went together to the cave in the hillside. But no Tammylan was there. The cave was empty.

"Bother!" said Penny. "Where do you suppose he is?"

"Look! Isn't that Tammylan down there!" said Benjy, his sharp eyes spying someone far off. "Yes, it is. He's near the pond where I fell in that day, Penny. Come on."

52

They ran down the hillside and made their way to where Tammylan was sitting. As they came near he held up his hand to stop them—but it was too late. They saw the quick movement of some animal—and it was gone.

"Oh, sorry, Tammylan," said Benjy. "I didn't know."

"He'll come back again," said Tammylan. "Hallo, Penny. Is your arm quite better now?"

"Yes, thank you," said Penny. "What was the creature that will come back again, Tammylan?"

"A snake," said Tammylan. Penny gave a cry of horror.

"Oh! A snake! Really and truly? Oh, don't let it come back. It will sting me."

"Don't be so silly, Penny," said Tammylan, in such a cross voice that Penny felt really hurt. "Snakes don't sting—they bite. And this one doesn't even bite. But you don't need to wait for it unless you want to. Go away and play, and Benjy and I will wait for it to come back."

Penny stared at Tammylan. "I thought snakes were horrid creatures," she said. "People always shiver when they talk about snakes. I've always been afraid of them."

"Well, go on being afraid of them then," said Tammylan. "If you prefer to shiver when you hear snakes spoken of, shiver! What about you, Benjy?"

"Oh, I want to stay, please," said Benjy eagerly. "I want to know how snakes get along without feet. I want to know how they get out of their skins. I . . ."

"So do I," said Penny, blinking away tears. "You needn't be so cross with me, Tammylan. I was only saying what other people said."

"And that's the silliest thing in the world to do!" said Tammylan, stretching out his hand and pulling the little girl down beside him. "Don't listen to what other people *say*. Find out things for yourself. They say snakes sting, do they? Well, find out from someone who really *knows*. You'll be telling me you're frightened of spiders next."

Now Penny *was* afraid of spiders—but she was even more afraid of telling Tammylan so at that moment. So she said nothing, but sat on the sunny ground beside him.

Presently there was a tiny rustling noise nearby and a long snake came softly up to Tammylan, wriggling his body from side to side. Penny was so excited that she quite forgot to do what she had felt sure she *would* do— and that was shiver. She sat just as still as the others.

Tammylan began to whistle to the snake. It looked at him out of wide-open eyes. Benjy saw that the eyes had no eye-lids, so the snake couldn't possibly shut its eyes even if it wanted to!

The snake put out its black tongue and ran it quickly over Tammylan's brown hand. It was a queer tongue, forked into two branches at the tip. Penny gave a scream.

"It's putting out its sting!" she cried. The snake hissed, and began to glide away. Tammylan whistled gently and softly and it slowly came back, putting its forked tongue in and out.

"You are a silly little girl, Penny," said Tammylan. "That is only the snake's tongue. It uses it to feel things— it likes to run its tongue over its food before it eats it, to feel its shape. It is split into two at the end to help it to feel things easily—its forked tongue is like two sensitive fingers. Don't let me hear you call it a sting again."

"No, Tammylan," said Penny, glad that the wild man was not really angry with her. Benjy put his hand slowly towards Tammylan's. The snake flickered its quick tongue over his fingers. Benjy's face was a sight to behold. It was shining with joy! To think that a snake would be friendly enough to do that to him!

54

"This is a grass snake, a great friend of mine," said Tammylan. "For three years it has come to me. Look at it well. Its family are ill-used by man, for people kill it whenever they see it."

"Oh why?" asked Benjy, remembering to keep his voice low.

"Like Penny here, they think all snakes are terrible!" said Tammylan. "This pretty grass snake is perfectly harmless. It has no poison. It never attacks anyone, not even the smallest child. It is a harmless, friendly creature. Look at its large eyes, Penny, with its round pupils circled with gold. Look at its pretty patches of orange just behind the head, rather like a bright collar."

Penny and Benjy looked. The snake looked back at them. Penny began to feel that it was rather a nice creature after all.

"It's a good long snake," said Benjy, looking at it.

"Just over three feet I should think," said Tammylan. "The female snakes are even longer. Grass snakes are graceful things—their bodies taper gradually from the waist to the tip of the tail. See its long narrow head, and look at the lovely patterning of spots and bars along its olive-brown back. Touch its body, Benjy, and feel the curious scales that cover its body, overlapping each other."

Benjy touched the snake and felt the scales. Penny hardly dared to and Tammylan did not make her. The snake drew back at Benjy's touch but did not go away.

"Where has it been all the winter?" asked Benjy. "Snakes sleep in the winter, don't they?"

"Yes," said Tammylan. "This one slept curled up with two or three others among some underground roots. The hot sun of the last day or two has awakened them. Ah—our snake spies a meal!"

The snake suddenly slid down the bank and entered the water. To the children's enormous astonishment it swam easily in the pond.

"Gracious! I didn't know snakes swam!" said Penny. "Whatever next?"

The snake had seen the movements of frogs and toads in the water. It caught one and brought it back to the bank, its scales glistening with water.

"The frog can't escape once it is in the snake's mouth," said Tammylan. "It has teeth that point backwards!"

"Look!" said Benjy, in excitement, "Is that another snake, Tammylan — just over there?"

"Yes!" said Tammylan. "Your eyes are getting sharp, Benjy. It's a smooth snake this time. If you felt its scales you would not feel the roughness that you felt when you touched the grass snake."

"Tammylan, whatever is it doing?" asked Penny. "It is pushing its head against that stone. Is it hurt?"

"Oh no!" said Tammylan. "It is just going to take off its skin, that's all."

Penny stared at Tammylan to see if he were joking. "But why should it take off its skin?" she asked in astonishment. "I never take mine off."

"No, because yours grows as *you* grow," said Tammylan. "But there are creatures whose bodies grow and whose skins don't — and then they have to take off their tight skins and wear others they have grown underneath. Watch this smooth snake and you will see it take off its whole skin, just as you might take off a stocking, inside-out."

The smooth snake rubbed its head against the rough stone until the skin was loose. Then, when the head-skin was off, the snaked glided out of the rest of its body-skin, turning it neatly inside-out as he went! The children stared in amazement.

Penny gave a shout. "Can I have the skin?"

The snake gave a frightened glance round and glided away into the undergrowth.

"You are a silly, Penny," grumbled Benjy. "Now you've frightened the smooth snake away and I wanted to feel its smooth body."

Tammylan picked up the snake-skin. He showed it to the children. "It's called a slough," he said. "See how perfect it is—even to the eye-covering! You were very lucky to see such a thing to-day. It is few people who see a snake casting its skin."

Benjy looked at the skin carefully. "However does a snake get along?" he asked. "It hasn't any feet at all, has it?"

"Not one," said Tammylan. "But it manages very well indeed without them—it walks on the free ends of its many ribs! It puts a few of them forward, pressing on the skin—then others behind follow—and then the rest—then the front ribs move forward again, and so on. So it performs that curious gliding movement which is really fascinating to watch."

"Are there any more snakes in our country besides the smooth snake and the grass snake?" asked Penny.

"Yes—one more—and a poisonous one this time!" said Tammylan. "Come with me and I'll show you one."

Penny wasn't at all sure that she wanted to go. "I don't want to be stung—I mean bitten," she said in a low voice.

"You won't be stung *or* bitten," said Tammylan. "But don't come if you don't want to. You come, Benjy."

Well, of course, as soon as Penny was told that she needn't come, she wanted to! So off they went, leaving the pond behind, and climbing the warm southern side of the heather-covered hill. Tammylan sat down. His sharp eyes had caught sight of a movement. He began to whistle what Benjy secretly called his 'snake-tune'. Benjy was already trying to practise it in his mind, hoping that he too would be able to call snakes from all over the place, just as Tammylan seemed to do.

There was a rustle near them. Penny and Benjy saw a short, thick-looking snake gliding up to the wild man. It was only about two feet long, and its coppery-red eye looked unwinkingly at Tammylan.

It was a brownish snake, with a line zigzagging down the middle of its back. On its head was a mark that looked like a V. Its tongue flickered out as it came.

"I don't like this snake so much as the others," said Penny.

"It isn't so pretty, certainly," said Tammylan, letting the snake feel his fingers with its tongue. "Its body is not so long and graceful – and do you see the mark on its head, rather like a V. V for viper – or A for adder if you look at it the other way! This snake is a viper or adder – our only poisonous snake."

"How does it bite, Tammylan?" asked Benjy, staring at the snake.

"Watch, Benjy, what the snake does when I show him this stick," said Tammylan. "Watch carefully."

The children watched. Tammylan picked up a short stick and brought it suddenly in front of the snake's head. In a trice it reared up its head, opened its mouth and showed two large teeth or fangs. It struck – and its fangs bit the stick. Tammylan laughed, and threw away the wood. He whistled his snake-tune again and the snake wavered its head to and fro in the air, quite peaceful and happy once more.

"Did you see those two fangs?" asked Tammylan after a moment. "Well, those were the poison-fangs. They lie back in the mouth usually, but when the snake wants to strike they get into position for biting, and bite like lightning."

"Where is the poison — is it on the fangs?" asked Benjy, staring at the snake.

"No — it is kept in a kind of bag or gland at the base of the tooth. When the fang strikes an enemy, and so presses on the bag of poison, it squeezes some out — and this runs down a passage in the fang, and into the wound made by the bite. So you see," said Tammylan, "a snake bites — but does not sting!"

"I shall be afraid of coming out on the hillside in case a viper bites me," said Penny fearfully.

"They rarely bite," said Tammylan, "and anyway, you are sensible enough to wear shoes, aren't you? Barefoot people, who might accidentally tread on a sleeping viper might possibly get bitten — but you may be sure that in the usual way a viper hears you coming long before you get to him, and slides away to safety. He is far more afraid of you than you are of him!"

A dog barked in the distance — and the viper at once glided off without a sound.

"There!" said Tammylan. "You see how the least noise sends it to hiding? You need not be afraid, Penny. And now I think it is time you went home, or your Uncle Tim will be coming after the wild man with a gun!"

The children laughed.

"Who can I bring next time?" asked Benjy.

"You can bring both the others," said Tammylan. "And you may ask your aunt if she will let you come at night, next week, when the moon is up."

"Ooh—what fun!" said Benjy.

"Can't I come too?" asked Penny, thinking that a moonlight adventure sounded very thrilling.

"Not this time," said Tammylan, "but you may keep the snake's cast-off skin for yourself, because you were quite a sensible little girl after all, and didn't run away when the snakes came!"

Penny was very pleased. How the others would envy her the snake's skin! She thanked Tammylan very much for it, and Benjy took her hand to take her home.

All the way home Benjy whistled a queer little tune. Penny looked at him in surprise.

"What tune is that?" she asked.

"It's the snake-tune that Tammylan whistled," said Benjy. "I'm going to practise it and call the snakes to me for all the others to see."

Well, when the others heard of the snakes and saw the snake's cast-off skin, and heard Benjy's queer whistle they were thrilled. "Auntie Bess! Benjy can whistle snakes to him!" cried Sheila. "Come and listen!"

So everybody sat still near Benjy whilst the boy whistled the queer monotonous tune—but alas, no snakes came at all, much to Auntie Bess's relief. Only Shadow, the collie, came rushing up and licked Benjy wetly on the nose.

"Don't, Shadow! Do you think you're a snake, you silly dog?" cried Benjy crossly. "Now you've spoilt my whistle!"

"And a good thing too!" said Auntie Bess. "I don't really feel that I want my farmyard full of snakes just at present, with all my young chicks about! Come along and have your meal, all of you. The cats will be eating it, if we don't go in and have it soon!"

IX

A MOONLIGHT ADVENTURE

Rory and Sheila were wildly excited when they heard that they were to go and see Tammylan in the moonlight.

"What friends will come to see him in the moonlight?" said Sheila. "Foxes, do you think—or otters?"

"Maybe badgers," said Rory. "Look—here's a picture of a badger, Sheila, in this book of Benjy's. Isn't he a queer-looking creature?"

All the children looked at the picture. "He's got such a funny face," said Rory. "Striped white and black—very easy to see! If he comes out at night I could see him a mile off in the moonlight!"

Auntie Bess wouldn't let the children go until a really warm night came. The moon rose bright, and the countryside was flooded with light. The three children were so excited. Penny was sad.

"Well, Penny, don't forget you've got a real snake's cast-off skin," said Benjy. "That ought to make up to you for anything!"

Penny cheered up. The others were not likely to see a snake throwing off its skin that night—and anyway they would tell her all that happened. Uncle Tim had promised to let her help him wash the new-laid eggs for a treat, and Penny was looking forward to that after breakfast the next day.

Benjy, Rory, and Sheila set off to Tammylan's cave. Tammylan was sitting outside with some of his friends. The children saw that they were rabbits, who fled as they came near.

"I wish animals wouldn't run away from us," said Sheila. "Hallo, Tammylan—we're so excited. What are we going to see to-night?"

"I hope you will see the gentleman who gave his name to our woods," said Tammylan, showing his white teeth in a smile.

"What gentleman?" asked Sheila puzzled.

"Master Brock, the Badger," said Tammylan. "Years ago the badger was far more plentiful here than he is now, and his country name of brock was given to our woods. He has been sleeping fast this cold winter, but now he should be about. Come along."

"Do you know where he lives, then?" asked Benjy, trotting along beside Tammylan.

"I know where all the badgers live in Brock Woods," said Tammylan, with a laugh. "Look—there goes the red fox, out on his evening hunt. I hope he is not after your uncle's chickens!"

In the moonlight, outlined against the bright sky, the three children could see the graceful figure of a fox on the side of the hill. He stood there, listening and sniffing.

"He can smell *me*—but he can smell you too," said Tammylan. "If I were alone he would come trotting at my heels, like a dog."

Benjy sighed enviously. "He's rather like a beautiful, bushy-tailed dog to look at, isn't he?" he said. "Oh—he's gone."

They made their way deep into Brock Woods. Soon they came to a big bank, and Tammylan stopped. An owl hooted loudly and made Sheila jump.

"Speak quietly now," said Tammylan. "Stand over here, so that the wind blows from the bank to us, then the badger will not smell us."

The children stared at the bank. In it, showing clearly in the moonlight, was a very dark hole, quite big.

"That is the doorway to the badger's 'sett', or 'den'," said Tammylan. "He may come out in a few minutes. We will watch for him."

Outside the badger's den was a big mound. "What's that?" whispered Sheila.

"That is the earth that the badger turned out when he dug his hiding-place," said Tammylan, in a voice like the wind in the trees. It was marvellous the way he could make words sound like the wind blowing.

"And what's that huge pile of old leaves over there?" whispered Rory.

"That is old bedding of the badger's," said Tammylan. "In the autumn he collects a great many dead leaves and takes them into his den for bedding. They keep him warm and cosy. But if he wakes up to have a little stroll in a warm spell he often turns out his bedding and brings in fresh."

"Oh look—look!" whispered Sheila, clutching hold of Tammylan's arm. "Something's coming out of the hole!"

Sure enough something was! A striped face looked out and sniffed the night air. It was Brock the Badger.

Not one of the four made a sound or a movement. The badger put his head out a little farther, and sniffed loudly. He was sniffing for the smell of enemies. He never came out if he smelt anything strange or frightening.

The wind was blowing from him to the children, so he could not smell them. Neither could they smell him, for their noses were not trained to smell the scent of animals' bodies. But Tammylan could smell him. Tammylan knew the smell of badgers and he liked it, for they were cleanly beasts. Tammylan sniffed Brock—but the badger could not sniff Tammylan's smell because of the wind.

The badger shuffled right out of his "sett" and the children could see him clearly in the moonlight — but as he went into the shadows he seemed to disappear!

"How funny!" whispered Sheila. "I can't see that striped face of his now. It seems to have gone — and yet I know he's there among those shadows, because I can hear him."

"His face is striped like that so that he may not easily be seen in the moonlit wood," said Tammylan, in his low voice. "For the same reason the zebra is striped, Sheila. White and black stripes look like white moonlight and black shadows. Now, here he comes, look — see his stout body and his rough, reddish-grey coat. Look at his pointed muzzle. Brock! Brock!"

The badger stopped dead and looked towards Tammylan. He sniffed hard and smelt the smell of the children as well as of his friend. He turned to go lumbering back to his sett. Then Tammylan spoke badger language — grunts and curious noises that Benjy knew he would never be able to make if he tried all his life long! The badger paused and looked doubtfully at Tammylan.

Tammylan left the children and went alone to Brock. The badger rolled over on his back like a dog and gave a grunt of pleasure as Tammylan knelt beside him to poke him and prod him just where he liked it most. The children hardly dared to breathe at such an extraordinary sight.

Tammylan spoke to the badger, and grunted to him, and in between he spoke to the children in the same kind of voice. "See his big claws, children? See how black he is underneath! See what a stout, broad body he has, this little badger of mine?"

Benjy could bear it no longer. He felt as if he must join in or burst. Surely, surely the badger would let him tickle it and tease it as Tammylan was doing?

He ran forward to join in the game — but before he reached the badger it had gone, and Tammylan was kneeling there alone! Benjy could hear the badger making its way through the wood. "Oh!" he said, disappointed. "It's gone."

"Of course!" said Tammylan. "Did you expect to do in one minute what has taken me years? And surely you know that no animal, wild or tame, will stand a rush like

67

that! Even Shadow, the collie, would have jumped to his feet!"

"Yes—I know," said Benjy. "But oh, Tammylan, I wanted to touch that badger so much. How did you manage to make it so tame?"

"I once had three badger cubs," said the wild man. "When they grew, they left me to live their own lives. That was one of the grown cubs. They still know me and are friends with me. Come nearer to Brock's den, children. Look inside. You cannot see much—but it is a big place if only you could get in and see!"

"How big is it?" asked Rory, kneeling down and almost putting his head inside.

"Rory's going in to look!" said Sheila, with a laugh. "Mind you don't meet two or three more badgers, Rory!"

"This sett goes in about nine or ten feet," said Tammylan. "There are passages and galleries too, and Master Brock has provided himself with a convenient back entrance right away at the back there, behind those bushes. I believe the red fox used to live in one of the passages, but the badger turned him out. He hates the fox's smell."

"Good gracious! It's a real underground house!" said Rory. "I do wish I was small enough to go in it. Where has the badger gone, Tammylan?"

"To find some food," said Tammylan. "He has slept nearly all the winter, and he is hungry. He blocks up this entrance and the back entrance too, when he goes to sleep."

"I should have thought he was too clumsy to hunt his food properly," said Benjy.

"He usually picks up wounded or ill animals," said Tammylan. "I know where Master Brock has gone to-night, I am sure. He has gone down to the rookery not far from your uncle's farm to see if any young rook has fallen from its nest!"

"Is he ever caught in a trap?" said Rory.

"Not very often," said Tammylan, leading the children away from the badger's home. "The badger that you saw to-night will never, I am sure, be caught in any trap. He has a curious way of dealing with traps."

"What's that?" asked Benjy.

"He rolls heavily on them!" said Tammylan. "He waits till he hears the spring go, then he knows the trap is safe. After that he calmly takes the bait and walks off with it!"

"He is cleverer than he looks!" said Sheila, admiringly. "Are you going to show us anything else to-night, Tammylan?"

"Only the way home," said Tammylan, with a chuckle. "There it is—look! Come and see me again another day some of you."

Then, off they went back to the farm in the moonlight, keeping a good look out for badgers and foxes and any other creatures that might come along. As for Benjy he tried to make the badger noises that Tammylan had made—until the others said he would have to buy them cotton-wool to put in their ears if he didn't stop!

X

TAMMYLAN'S TREE-HOUSE

One morning, when the children went down to breakfast, they heard Auntie Bess grumbling. "My nice lawn is quite spoilt," she said. "Just look at it!"

The children looked out at the grass. It was a nice lawn, and their aunt was proud of it. But this morning it certainly looked very queer.

"It's all up and down!" said Penny, in surprise. "It looks as if someone has made tunnels underneath and thrown up little hills and banks all over it. What's happened, Auntie Bess?"

"You'd better ask your friend Tammylan!" said Uncle Tim, looking up from his newspaper. "I've no doubt he would call up a whole lot of the little wretches who have spoilt the lawn, and let them tell you a wonderful tale — but all *I* can say is — I'm going to get the mole-catcher here and tell him to trap the little pests who are mining under my lawns and my fields too!"

"Oh — so moles did it?" said Rory. "Well, I've never seen the work of moles before. I don't even know what they are like to look at."

"I do," said Benjy. "They are made for tunnelling, aren't they, Uncle Tim? Their front paws are really spades."

"Spades!" said Penny, in surprise. "Do you mean real spades like we have when we go to the sea?"

The others laughed. "Don't be such a baby, Penny," said Rory. "Benjy means the paws *act* like spades. We'll go and see Tammylan this morning and ask him a few questions."

"And tell him that if he can find any good words for moles as far as farmers are concerned I'll be surprised!" said Uncle Tim. "Pesky little creatures!"

The children were pleased to have an excuse to go and see Tammylan. They had been busy at the farm for two or three weeks, and when they *had* gone to see their friend he was nowhere to be found. Perhaps they would be luckier to-day. So after they had done their various jobs of feeding the farmyard creatures, washing the eggs, and giving fresh water to hens and others, the children set off to find the wild man.

But again the cave was empty, and again there was no sign of Tammylan. The children were disappointed. "Perhaps he isn't wild any more. Perhaps he has gone tame," said Penny.

Sheila giggled. "You do say silly things, Penny," she said.

The sun shone down warmly. Chaffinches carolled madly, and larks sang their sibilant song high in the sky. The music came dropping round the children as they stood wondering about Tammylan.

"I like the larks," said Sheila, looking up at them. "If I were a bird I'd fly as high as I could to sing. Listen to that lark—you can almost catch his song as it comes tumbling down from the sky!"

Penny put out her hands to catch the notes of the song, and the others laughed at her. "Come on," said Rory. "We can't stay here all morning. Let's wander round a bit and yell. Perhaps Tammylan will hear us calling and shout back."

So every now and again they shouted for Tammylan—and at last, away in the distance, they heard an answering cry.

"That's old Tammylan!" cried Benjy in delight, and the four children raced off over heather and bracken to where the call had sounded. Tammylan sent his call at intervals to guide them — and soon they came to his hiding-place.

It was by a backwater of the river — a quiet peaceful place, where moor-hens bobbed about, and fishes jumped for flies. "A Tammylanny sort of place," Benjy thought to himself.

Their friend was there, and on his shoulder was a red squirrel, with a bushy tail and bright black eyes. When they saw the squirrel the children stopped their rush and walked quietly. They had learnt enough of animals now to know that even the tamest ones hated too sudden an arrival.

The red squirrel did not leave Tammylan's shoulder. Tammylan smiled at the children. "Hallo," he said. "I wondered where you had all got to. I haven't seen you for some time."

"We've been helping our uncle and aunt," said Rory, "and when we *did* come to find you, we couldn't. But now we have, and I'm glad."

Tammylan was very busy at something. Penny looked hard at what he was doing. "Tammylan!" she cried. "Are you making a house?"

"Yes — a tree-house!" said Tammylan. "I always live in a tree-shelter in the warm months of the year. This is the house I made two years ago — I am just trimming it up to make it right for me again now."

"But the house is growing!" said Sheila, looking at it. "Oh, Tammylan, do you really live in a growing house?"

"Why not?" said Tammylan. "If my walls grow buds and my roof grows leaves, so much the better!"

It was a most extraordinary house. Tammylan had planted quick-growing willows close to one another, and used their trunks for the walls. He had trained the top of their branches across for a roof! Between the trunks of the willows he had woven long, pliable willow twigs, and had stuffed up all the cracks with heather and moss. It was the cosiest house imaginable.

But it was alive and growing! That was what amazed the children. The roof was green with leaves. Buds and leaves grew from the walls too. Tammylan was busy trimming the twigs and branches to make his house neat.

"Oh, if only I could have helped you to build your

house!" said Benjy. "I wish I had a growing house like that. Where's the door, Tammylan?"

"There is no door," said Tammylan. "The south side is open to the wind and the sun. There is a flat screen of woven twigs over there, which I use to shut up the house occasionally—but I do not need a door."

The backwater of the river flowed by Tammylan's house, murmuring as it went. Primroses grew almost to the doorway. Bluebells pushed up all around it. The four children looked and looked—it was like a house in a fairy-tale.

Penny went quietly into the house. There was nothing inside but a few pots and an old rug. "Are you going to have a bed, Tammylan?" she called.

"You can make me one if you like, Penny," said Tammy-lan. "All I want is plenty of dry heather. It smells so sweet at night!"

"Penny can make you your bed soon," said Sheila, undoing a packet she carried. "We'll have something to eat first. Look, Tammylan—chocolate cake baked by my Auntie Bess yesterday. It's for our lunch. Will you share it?"

"I should love to," said Tammylan, seeing that there was a whole cake there. He took out his knife and cut it into enormous slices. "Let's sit down by the river and have a talk."

The little red squirrel had been sitting on Tammylan's shoulder all the time. When it saw the cake it made a little chittering noise.

"You don't like cake, Bushy!" said Tammylan. The squirrel took a bit of cake, bounded off Tammylan's shoulder, and disappeared with its prize behind a tree.

"He'll come back," said Tammylan, seeing Benjy's

disappointed face. "And probably bring a friend too, if I know anything about Master Bushy."

The children hoped he would. They munched their delicious chocolate cake and talked to Tammylan.

"Tammylan, Uncle is very cross because moles have tunnelled across his lawn," said Benjy. "He said he'd be surprised if even *you* could find a good word to say for moles where farmers were concerned."

"Really?" said Tammylan. "Well, we'll see. Finish your cake and we'll go and pay a call on a few moles I know."

Penny almost choked in her excitement. Really, you couldn't mention *any*thing to Tammylan without hearing that some creature or other was his friend.

"I believe that if you lived in a jungle all the tigers would follow you round like dogs!" she said, with her mouth full.

"I should feel a bit uncomfortable with tigers behind me all day long," said Tammylan, laughing. "Have you finished? Well, come along then."

Just as they were leaving, the red squirrel came bounding back—and with him were two other red squirrels, their bushy tails streaking out behind them.

"Too late, Bushy, too late!" said Tammylan, shaking his head. "The cake's all gone."

"No, it isn't, Tammylan, no it isn't!" cried Benjy. "I saved a bit in *case* Bushy did bring a friend. Here's a bit of cake, squirrels!"

To Benjy's joy all three squirrels scampered up to his outstretched hand. One stood on his hind legs and sniffed at the cake. One jumped on to Tammylan's shoulder—and oh, my goodness me, the third one actually ran all the way up Benjy's back and sat on the nape of his neck! Benjy was so thrilled that he couldn't move. He just stood there, half-bent, his eyes shining.

"Well, Benjy seems to have turned into a statue!" said Tammylan, with a laugh. "Come on, Benjy—the squirrel will stick on all right if you walk! He likes you."

"Oh, I wish he'd like me too!" cried Penny. And Rory and Sheila wished the same. Benjy began to walk—a bit stiffly at first, in case the squirrel took fright and bounded away. Then, as he got used to feeling the warm furry bundle at his neck, he walked properly, and the squirrel balanced itself easily.

"The third one's gone," said Penny. "I wish it had stayed with us and let me carry it."

They left the strange growing house behind them, and followed Tammylan. He led them away from the river to a grassy field—and there, all around them, were the hills and tunnels of many moles.

"And now we'll catch a little velvet miner, and see what he's got to say for himself!" said Tammylan.

THE VELVET-COATED MINER

The sun shone down hotly on the field. There was a bank nearby where primroses grew in big patches of yellow, and where white violets scented the air. Tammylan sat down on the bank and the children sat by him. The two squirrels sat still, their bright eyes watching everything.

"Now," said Tammylan. "There are moles at work here. I saw their work when I came by this morning. If we sit quite still for a while, we shall see the earth being thrown up, and maybe I can get a mole for you to see. Keep quiet now."

So they all sat as quiet as mice. Tammylan's squirrel sniffed and sniffed at Penny's hair, and the little girl was delighted. The sniffing tickled her, but she didn't move. Benjy's squirrel kept brushing the boy's ear with his whiskers, and it felt lovely.

Suddenly Tammylan pointed. The field was ridged here and there with the tunnels of the moles and with small hills of earth—but as the children watched, a new ridge appeared bit by bit. The grass seemed to be forced upwards as if something was tunnelling underneath and pushing it up.

"There's a mole at work there," said Tammylan. "He's not far under the surface either. The soil is rich and soft just here so the moles do not go very deep. Keep still and I'll get him for you."

What happened next the children found it difficult to see because it all came so quickly. Tammylan knelt down by the newly made run, just at the end of it. There was a scraping and scrabbling—and then Tammylan turned round, his hands covered with earth—and in them a struggling little body dressed in grey-black velvet! It made no sound at all and the children crowded round to see it.

"Quiet, little Mowdie Mole," said Tammylan, stroking the struggling body with his strong brown hand. In a moment or two the mole stopped wriggling and lay quite quiet. The two red squirrels, after a disgusted sniff at the mole, tore back to the woods, much to Benjy's dismay.

"Here is our little miner!" said Tammylan. "Stroke him. Feel his soft velvet coat. See how the hairs grow, thickly and straight up. They do not lie all one way as a dog's hairs do, or a cat's. He can go either forwards or backwards as he pleases, you see, without his coat being ruffled up the 'wrong way'. That is important to him in his tunnelling underground."

"Where are his eyes?" asked Penny, stroking the fat little miner.

"Buried deep in his fur," said Tammylan. "He has no use for them underground, and he rarely comes above the surface. But look at the most important part of him—his front paws."

Penny looked at them, still half-expecting to see a sort of seaside spade! She saw a pair of wide-open hands, the palms facing outwards for digging. They were very large hands, for such a small creature, and they were set with big strong nails for digging. Penny could just imagine how well the mole could use them in the earth.

Rory touched the strong little spade-hands gently. At once they moved as if they were digging, and the long snout quivered and shook.

"What a long loose nose he's got," said Sheila. "What does he use that for? Smelling out his food?"

"Yes—and to turn up the earth when he has loosened it with his paws," said Tammylan. "When you saw him tunnelling just now, he was loosening the earth and then forcing it upwards with his snout—and so you saw the ridge of earth appearing on the surface of the field. He has a good sense of smell too, and finds his nose very useful indeed."

The mole began to wriggle again and Tammylan stroked it gently. "We'll put him down here, where the earth is soft," he said. "Then little Mowdie Mole will show you how he can use his spades!"

Tammylan put the mole down—and at once it set to work digging in the soft earth. How it dug with those spade-like hands! The earth seemed to sink away under the mole—and in a very short while the velvet-coated creature had gone completely underground!

"I wish I could do that!" said Rory. "Just dive into the earth and disappear! It looks so easy!"

"What does the mole look for when it tunnels?" asked Penny. "And why does it tunnel, Tammylan? Does it like living in the dark, under the ground?"

"It doesn't think about whether it likes it or not," said Tammylan. "Its food is there—and to get it, it must tunnel through the earth! It eats earthworms, and grubs of all kinds—the leather-jackets, the cockchafer grubs, the harmful wireworms—and if it smells snails or slugs above ground it will come up and get those too!"

"Does the mole have a nest or a den?" asked Rory, watching another ridge appearing in the field, and wondering if it was made by their little mole.

"Yes—he makes a nice little nest for himself," said Tammylan. "I'll show you where there is one on the way back. It is quite a big hill, as you will see."

"Isn't it funny to think that moles are making a sort of underground world below our feet?" said Sheila. "I suppose the people who made the Underground Railway copied the moles and the rabbits."

"I shouldn't be surprised," said Tammylan. "You know, the moles have their own system of main roads and highways in the fields — ways which they know as well as you know your own roads. From these highways they branch off in their hunting, making new tunnels to find food. But they come back to the main roads whenever they want to. I have sometimes dug into a mole's highway, and they are just about the size of the mole's body, and are worn quite smooth and hard by the continual passage of hurrying moles!"

"A real little world of their own!" said Benjy, wishing he were small enough to go hurrying along a mole's road, down the side-roads, up the tunnels, and see whom he would meet. "Where's that mole's nest, Tammylan?"

"Come along and look," said their friend, and the children followed him down the field. Tammylan stopped and pointed to a bush. Half-hidden under the brambles was a hill of earth, about a foot high and about three feet across. "That is where our velvet-coated friend nests," said Tammylan. "Inside you would find his sleeping-chamber, and above it little tunnels leading upwards, through which he pushed the earth he dug out when he made his nest. This hill is made of the earth. He is a clever little fellow, isn't he?"

"Yes," said Rory, wishing he could see inside the hillock. "Well, I think I shall know what these hills of earth are now, when I see them again! I saw one the other day and couldn't think what it was."

"You must go now," said Tammylan. "It's getting late."

The children ran off—but they hadn't gone far before Benjy stopped. "Bother!" he said. "Tammylan didn't tell us what to tell Uncle Tim—surely there must be good things to say to a farmer about a mole?"

"Well, we can't go back and ask Tammylan now," said Rory impatiently. "We shall be late. Surely we can think of something for ourselves. We know all about moles!"

So all of them thought hard as they went home. Uncle Tim was in the farmyard, on his way in to his lunch.

"Well!" he said. "Have you been mole-hunting?"

"Yes!" said Rory. "We've seen a mole, and how it digs."

"It wears a velvet coat, Uncle!" cried Penny.

"And has Tammylan any good to say about the tiresome little creature?" said Uncle Tim with a laugh. "I've been to the mole-catcher this morning, and he'll be along soon with his traps."

"We forgot to ask Tammylan what to tell you," said Benjy, "but Uncle, the mole catches earthworms—isn't that a good thing for you?"

"No," said Uncle Tim at once. "Earthworms are good for our fields."

"Oh," said Benjy. "Well, what about leather-jackets and wireworms and grubs?"

"Ah, now you're talking!" said Uncle Tim. "Yes—I'm thankful to any creature that eats those pests for me. They ruin many a good crop!"

"And Uncle, they make tunnels everywhere under the fields!" cried Rory. "Surely that must help to drain them!"

"Quite true," said Uncle Tim.

"And I should think it's very good for your land to have the under-soil thrown up to the air," said Benjy solemnly. "It must air it nicely."

Uncle Tim shouted with laughter. "You'll make a

farmer yet, Benjy!" he said. "Come along in. You've said some sensible things to me — but all the same I'm going to rid my land of the moles if I have to have the mole-catcher here every week!"

But what do you think Tammylan said when Benjy told him that? He said, "No mole-catcher ever yet got rid of all the moles in a field, Benjy — and never will!"

"Why doesn't he?" asked Benjy. "Can't he?"

"He may catch all the grown moles!" Tammylan said. "But *he leaves the youngsters in the mother mole's nest.* Would a mole-catcher rob himself of his living, Benjy? No, no — there are always some left to grow up and have families — and then the mole-catcher is sent for once again!"

And when the mole-catcher came to set his traps, Benjy comforted himself and thought of the many nests of baby moles scattered here and there under the ground. The youngsters would soon grow up, and then once more the highways under the fields would be alive with the smooth velvety bodies hurrying to and fro on their endless hunt for worms and grubs.

XII

AN EXCITING MORNING

The children settled down so well to their life at the farm that it began to seem years to them since they had left London. Their mother and father had sailed to America, and gay picture post cards kept arriving. At first these seemed very thrilling to the children and they wished they had gone to America, too — but soon the happenings at the farm began to seem far more important than things in faraway America.

By the end of May all the children had fat legs and rosy cheeks. Penny had grown such a lot that her aunt thought she really must get some more clothes for her.

"We'll send Penny back to London, and ask her friends there to take her to buy some new clothes," said Uncle Tim slyly. Penny gave a screech.

"I won't go back to London! I won't! I'll wear nothing but a bathing-suit. I don't want new clothes!"

All the same, something had to be done, so Penny and Sheila were put in the pony-trap and driven off to the nearest town to buy bigger clothes and shoes.

The boys were all right — their jerseys and shorts did not matter. So they were left at home, and as soon as they had done their jobs, they looked at one another.

"I vote we go and see old Tammylan," said Benjy. "I'm simply longing to feel a squirrel on my shoulder again! Shall we go?"

"Yes," said Rory, cleaning out a pail, and putting it back in its place. "We'll just tell Uncle. Perhaps we could take our dinner."

Jane, the cook, put them up a picnic lunch in a few minutes, and the boys set off. It was a lovely day and Brock Woods were still blue with bluebells. The gorse was blazing on the hillside, its yellow blossoms sending out a delicious smell.

"Vanilla!" said Rory.

"Hot coconut!" said Benjy. "Oh, look—there's a snake! Sh! Do keep quiet, Rory. I want to see if I can make it come to me!"

Rory stood perfectly still. Benjy began his "snake-whistle". It was a funny kind of whistle, and at first the snake seemed to listen. But then it uncoiled itself, gave Benjy a funny look out of its wide-open eyes, and glided softly away.

"You'll never be a snake-charmer!" said Rory, laughing at Benjy's cross face.

"It nearly came," said Benjy. "I saw it just thinking about it. It was a grass snake, like the first one that Penny and I saw."

Tammylan was not in his cave, so the boys made their way to the tree-house. It was as strange and as lovely as ever. The boys peered inside. Tammylan had a bed of heather now, and a few of his things were arranged neatly on a kind of shelf.

"Let's sit here and wait for Tammylan," said Benjy. "I'm tired."

So down they sat, leaning against the doorway of the little green house. The sun shone between the trees, and golden freckles of sunshine lay on the ground, moving as the wind shook the leaves above. It was all very peaceful and quiet.

Presently a moor-hen swam to the bank and clambered up on its strong legs. "How funny!" whispered Benjy. "It is a swimming bird but it hasn't got webbed feet!"

"Sh!" said Rory. "It's coming here!"

So it was. It came half-running, half-walking to the tree-house, as if to make a call on Tammylan. Then it suddenly saw the two boys and stopped. With a squawk it rushed back to the bank again, dived into the river — and disappeared!

"It's completely gone!" said Benjy, in astonishment. "Where is it? It must be under the water."

A series of small ripples began to show on the surface of the water, and soon made a little trail on the river. "It must be the moor-hen that is making that trail," said Benjy. "Oh look — it's stopped — and it's sticking just its beak out. Can you see it, Rory?"

"Yes," said Rory. "Keep quiet now, Benjy. Let's see if anything else comes. This is fun."

The boys sat quietly. Somewhere a warbler sang his quaint little song. Somewhere a blackbird fluted like a musician composing a new melody all for himself. The wind moved in the trees and the sun-freckles danced on the ground.

Rory nudged Benjy. Two bright black eyes were looking up at the boys from a tuft of long grass nearby. The eyes stared unwinkingly. The boys kept perfectly still. The eyes still stared — and then a brown nose came up and sniffed the air gently to get the smell of the boys. As soon as it smelt their scent, nose and eyes disappeared in a flurry and a tail appeared for half a moment, and then disappeared too.

"Another of Tammylan's friends, I suppose," whispered Benjy. "I wonder what it was. A mouse of some sort, I think."

"Sh! Look over there," whispered Rory, slightly

nodding his head to the right. Benjy looked. A wild duck in all the beauty of its early summer plumage had come from the water, and was preening itself in a patch of sunlight. The sun fell on its brilliant feathers, and the colours shone as brightly as a rainbow. The duck heard the boys and looked towards them. It thought that the noise was only Tammylan and the big bird settled down on the bank in the sun, tucked its head under its wing and slept.

A large fish leapt out of the water at a fly. The boys jumped at the splash. "Look at those funny flies, Benjy," whispered Rory. "They've got three tails, like stiff hairs, hanging down behind them. What are they?"

"May-flies," whispered back Benjy, proud that he knew. "Fish love them. Those must be early ones. Look — there goes another fish jumping at the flies. Do you see how the flies rise up in the air altogether when a fish jumps and then go down again altogether? It seems as if they are dancing, doesn't it?"

A robin flew down and looked sideways at the boys. He had bold black eyes, and he hopped nearer on his long thin legs. He opened his mouth, swelled out his throat and warbled such a rich little song that the two boys were enchanted. Then it flung a dead leaf over its shoulder, gave a kind of bow and bob, flicked its wings and flew to a near-by branch to keep watch.

"I say, Rory, wouldn't it be marvellous to live in a growing house like Tammylan does, and know all these creatures?" said Benjy longingly. "What shall we see next?"

They saw a baby rabbit! It had disobeyed orders and had come out in the daytime instead of waiting for the dusk. Maybe it wanted to speak to friend Tammylan — anyway, there it was, quite suddenly, almost at the boys' feet! It

looked at them out of big surprised eyes.

"*Oh!*" cried Benjy. "You're like a toy rabbit we've got at home! Come here — do come here!"

But Benjy's surprise was too much for the young rabbit. It disappeared as quickly as it had come, and the boys saw its white bobtail flash — and then it was gone.

A swan sailed by down the stream, its white wings curving about its back. Its head was held proudly and it looked with dignity from one side to the other.

"It reminds me of those old sailing-ships somehow," said Benjy. "Isn't it marvellous? Look at its big feet paddling it along at the back, Rory. They act like oars."

The swan heard Benjy's voice and looked enquiringly at the bank. Thinking that Tammylan was there, with a titbit for him, he sailed majestically to the grassy bank.

He shook his wings then clambered clumsily up the bank. He waddled up to the two boys.

To tell the truth, Rory was rather frightened. The swan was a very big bird, and he didn't much like it quite so near him. But Benjy, as usual, was only too delighted to have anything alive close to him. He made no movement except to slip a sandwich out of his lunch packet. He held it out to the swan with a slow movement.

The swan took it quickly in his beak. He dropped the sandwich on the ground, pecked at it, and then gulped it down. He looked up for more.

"Give him one of yours, Rory," said Benjy. But Rory was really rather afraid of the swan's beak! So Benjy gave him another of his own sandwiches.

The swan liked them. It wanted more. "Oh no, my dear, greedy, beautiful swan," said Benjy, reaching out his hand to run it softly down the swan's graceful neck. "I want my dinner, you know — and you've already had a good bit of it!"

The swan pecked at Benjy's packet of sandwiches, and broke the whole lot up! Benjy tried to save them but it was no use.

"Oh, Benjy! Make him go away!" said Rory, afraid that his own lunch would go too. "He's too greedy. Send him away."

"Well, how do you send a swan away without making it angry or frightened?" demanded poor Benjy, looking with dismay at his spoilt lunch. "Goodness! Now he's pecked my chocolate. Swan, go away. Go and swim on the river. You look beautiful there!"

The swan came even closer. Benjy wondered if he dared to push it away. He tried — but the swan had far more pushing power than Benjy. The boy rolled over.

Then Rory had a good idea. He took one of Benjy's sandwiches and threw it a little distance away. The swan waddled after it. Then Rory threw another sandwich a bit farther off. The swan went after that. And then there was no more of Benjy's lunch left, so Rory had to begin on his own! He took a sandwich and threw it into the water.

The swan looked at it, and turned and hissed at Rory as if to say, "Bad shot! Now I shall have to go in and get it!"

He slid down the grassy bank and entered the water with a splash. And at once he changed from a clumsy waddler into a graceful swimmer, and the boys watched him admiringly. Rory had to throw the swan half his lunch before the lovely white bird was satisfied and swam off down the river in a stately manner.

"Well!" said Rory. "I agree that it's fun to meet all Tammylan's friends—but I think, Benjy, I prefer the shy ones!"

"Tirry-lee!" said the robin from its branch, and it flew down almost on to Rory's foot, to peck up a crumb.

The boys watched it—and then they heard somebody laughing. The laughing went on—and then Benjy looked up and saw Tammylan lying on a branch up in a tree not far off!

"Tammylan!" he cried. "You've been there all the time!"

"Yes," laughed Tammylan. "I wanted to see how my friends liked you—but I couldn't help laughing at you and the swan. He liked you a bit too much, didn't he?"

"He liked our *lunch* too much," said Benjy, pulling a face. "We thought we had brought enough for you too, Tammylan—but now there isn't even enough for one of us."

"You shall have lunch with me to-day," said Tammylan, and he leapt lightly down from the tree. "I went out hunting this morning and I have found all kinds of strange and delicious roots, leaves and buds! Wait till I prepare them and cook them for you!"

The boys watched Tammylan peel roots of all colours and shapes. They saw him shred leaves into his pot. They knew none of them except young nettle leaves.

"Are we going to eat nettle leaves?" asked Benjy in dismay. "Won't they sting our tongues?"

"Wait and see!" said Tammylan, with a chuckle. "Look — suck this whilst you are waiting!"

He tossed the boys what looked like tender green shoots of rose briars. He had peeled them and taken off the thorns. The boys put them into their mouths, not really liking the idea of chewing them — but to their surprise they had a most delicious taste.

"I should never dare to chew stalks and leaves and roots in case I was poisoned," said Benjy.

"Quite right," said Tammylan, putting the pot over a fire he had made outside his green house. "A great many things are poisonous — and also a great many things are good and delicious to eat — but unless you know them, as I do, you must never make silly experiments."

They had a strange but delightful meal. There was enough chocolate left for them all to have, and it seemed that Tammylan was as fond of that as the two boys were.

"The girls have gone to buy new dresses," said Benjy. "They are like the animals and birds — want new clothes in the spring-time!"

"And very nice too," said Tammylan. "I love to see the birds put on their brilliant spring coats, and to see the animals freshen themselves up and become lively."

A chittering noise made the boys look up. A red squirrel sat on a branch above them. Tammylan smiled. "He is cross with me because I picked some of the juicy buds he loves for himself," said the wild man.

The squirrel gave a tiny bark and stamped on the bough with his feet. Then he bounded off.

"He is building a nest for his wife," said Tammylan. "Would you like to see it?"

"Oh *yes!*" said the boys, knowing that this meant climbing a tree. "Come on, Tammylan—where is it?"

XIII

TAMMYLAN'S SQUIRRELS

Tammylan led the way through the wood. The hazels and oaks gave way to pine-trees, standing rather dark and sombre in the summer sunshine. The boys saw three or four red squirrels racing about. Some were on the ground, others shot up into the trees.

"Watch how they leap from twig to twig!" said Tammylan. "See how clever and light-footed they are—they seem almost to fly without wings!"

Rory and Benjy stood and watched. The red squirrels chattered at them. Then two began to chase one another and they scampered through the trees, leaping from the end of one twig to the beginning of another without a pause.

"Don't they ever fall?" asked Benjy, in wonder. "What

happens when they miss their footing — or the twig breaks, Tammylan?"

"Watch and see," said Tammylan. "There — did you see that squirrel? He wanted to leap from one tree to another but the twig he sprang to broke beneath his foot! But did he fall?"

"No!" said Benjy. "He simply dropped to the next twig below — but that broke too — and he dropped to another — and that held — so off he went up the tree as quick as lightning!"

"They use their tails to help them to balance themselves, don't they?" asked Rory. "Aren't they quick and light? Oh, how I'd love to play about in the trees like that!"

"Look, Tammylan — what's the squirrel doing over there?" asked Benjy, nudging Tammylan. "Is he eating the grass?"

All three of them looked towards a patch of long green grass. The red squirrel that Benjy was speaking of was busy pulling up the grass with his front paws. He rolled it into a ball with his clever paws, and then stuffed it into his mouth.

"It *is* eating it!" said Benjy. "Gracious, it's pulling some more and stuffing it in!"

"It isn't eating it, Benjy. It is the squirrel's way of carrying it," said Tammylan. "He is going to take it to his nest, and make a cosy lining with it! He is pleased to find such nice long grass — it will make a good lining. And look — here comes another squirrel with his mouth full — what is sticking out of his lips?"

"It's hay in *his* mouth!" said Rory. "Has he been fetching hay for his nest?"

"Yes," said Tammylan. "He has evidently found a hay-stack near enough to rob, and he knows it makes a cosy lining! Now — what about looking at the nest itself, boys?"

"Oh yes!" cried Benjy. "Where is it?"

Tammylan led them to a fir tree. The boys looked up. Half-way to the top they saw a big erection of twigs.

"Can you climb this tree?" asked Tammylan. "The first part is rather straight. But you can use those old bits of broken boughs for your feet, if you feel them carefully before you put your weight on them."

"Of course we can climb the tree!" said Rory scornfully. "We may be Londoners, but we can climb all right!"

All the same Tammylan had to watch them at first, and give them a bit of a help. But when they were well up in the tree it was easy to climb. They came to the big nest — and a red squirrel appeared at the opening to the nest and gave tiny barks at them to make them go away!

"Now, now, Bushy!" said Tammylan in his low voice — and the squirrel quietened down and leapt to his shoulder. Nearby was another squirrel — Bushy's little wife. She chattered at them as they looked at her nest.

"See how well it is made," said Tammylan. "Sometimes squirrels use old nests made by birds — a magpie's perhaps — but this time Bushy has made one entirely himself. He has worked very hard!"

Benjy looked closely at it. "Are these bits of bark?" he asked, pulling out a thin strip.

"Yes — the squirrel strips off tree-bark with his sharp teeth and weaves it into his nest," said Tammylan. "And look — here is moss — and leaves. It is a fine nest. We call it a drey — did you know? A squirrel's drey."

"It's a pretty name," said Benjy, fingering the moss. "What's the drey like inside, Tammylan?"

"Feel and see," said Tammylan. So Benjy and then Rory put in their hands and felt the softness inside. It was well lined with grass—the grass that the boys had seen the squirrel pulling down below.

"This drey is dome-shaped, and has a roof," said Tammylan. "Sometimes they are cup-shaped, and then they are just resting-places. This will make a fine nursery for squirrel babies. It is a good sight to see four or five little bright-eyed squirrels peeping out of the nest-opening at me when I pass by!"

"I'm going down now," said Benjy. "Bushy, you can go into your drey! We've finished looking at it!"

Bushy was pleased. He waited till all three were down on the ground again, and then he and his wife popped into the big drey to make sure that no damage had been done!

"Last year Bushy made his nest in a big hole in the trunk of an old tree," said Tammylan. "But it was cut down in the autumn, so he had to find a new tree this year. He rested all the winter in an old drey in that tree nearby —but it wasn't suitable for a proper drey for himself and his wife. That is why he has been so busy this spring!"

"Do squirrels sleep all the winter through, as the snakes do?" asked Rory.

"Oh no!" said Tammylan, sitting down to watch the squirrels playing in the wood. "They only sleep when the weather is very bitter. They love to come out in a warm spell, even though snow may be on the ground! In fact, last winter they played in the snow just as you do—I half-expected them to roll up snowballs and throw them at me!"

The boys laughed. "What do they eat, then, if they wake up in the winter?" asked Rory. "They hide nuts, don't they?"

"Yes—nuts, beech-mast, acorns," said Tammylan. "But they often forget where they have hidden them. And sometimes the mice find them and take them away for themselves. It is funny to see an anxious squirrel scrabbling about in corners and under leaves for his hidden store — feeling quite sure he *did* put it there! And perhaps a bright-eyed mouse not far off watches him from a hole in a tree-trunk, knowing quite well that the nuts will never be found, because he has eaten them himself!"

"Do squirrels eat birds' eggs?" asked Benjy.

"Sometimes," said Tammylan. "And sometimes they are bold enough to carry young nestlings from the nest to eat, too. The wise mother-bird will never remain away from her nest too long in a wood where squirrels live — she knows her young ones will be in danger if she does."

"They like toadstools, too, don't they?" said Rory.

"Some kinds," said Tammylan. "You know, I love the edible toadstools myself, and . . ."

"Tammylan! But toadstools are deadly poison!" cried Benjy in horror.

"Some are poisonous, and some are good to eat," said Tammylan, smiling. "Don't you go trying any, though — you are sure to choose the poisonous kind! But I know which are safe, and I make many a delicious meal from them. You shall share some with me later on. But what I was saying was that sometimes when I go hunting for the particular toadstools that I love, the squirrels see that I am picking them, and they come and scold me — because, you see, they are what they want for themselves!"

"I'd like to see them scolding you!" said Benjy.

"They not only chatter at me, and stamp their tiny feet in anger on the tree branches above, but they even run down and scamper across to me — and help themselves out of my basket!" said Tammylan.

"Will you tell us when there are baby squirrels to be

seen?" asked Rory. "And, by the way, Tammylan — aren't there any *grey* squirrels in these woods? I've only seen the red ones. There were lots of grey ones in London, and they were very tame, too. But not nearly so pretty as these red ones."

"Those are descendants of American squirrels that were let loose in London years ago," said the wild man. "They have spread outwards, and now in many places they have driven away the little red squirrel. But we have not yet had any of the grey ones — and I hope we shan't, for I like my happy little red friends, and would hate to see them forced away by grey strangers!"

It was pleasant to sit in the woods, listening to the calls of the birds and watching the friendly squirrels at play. Bushy was on and off Tammylan's shoulder all the time, and his little wife visited Benjy, too. Rory was not so lucky. He could not remember not to make quick movements, so the little creatures avoided him. At last, seeing his disappointed face, Tammylan put Bushy on to Rory's shoulder.

Bushy sat there for two seconds, and Rory was delighted — but then the small creature was off and up a tree in a twinkling.

"Tammylan, I shall be eleven next week," said Benjy. "Aren't I getting old?"

"You are, rather," said Tammylan, looking at the boy, with a smile. "So you are going to have a birthday? Well, I wonder what birthday treat you would like from me?"

"Oh! I don't want a present or a treat!" said Benjy at once.

"Well, I'd like to give you a treat of some sort," said Tammylan. "Think now — you can choose."

Benjy thought. Then his face went red and he looked up

at Tammylan shyly. "Well," he said, and stopped. "Well, Tammylan . . ."

"Go on," said Tammylan. "Is it something so difficult?"

"Oh no," said Benjy. "You see . . ."

"*I* know what he wants to say!" said Rory, taking pity on Benjy. "He's often said it to us. He would like nothing better than to come and spend a night with you in your tree-house, Tammylan — and hear the night-owls hooting, and the splash of the river going by, and see the stars through the doorway of your house."

"Is that right, Benjy?" asked Tammylan, looking very pleased. Benjy nodded.

"I hope you don't think it's awful cheek," he said.

"Why should I?" asked Tammylan. "Very well — that shall be your birthday treat from me. Come any night next week, the warmer the better. It will be moonlight, and we will have a few visitors, I hope!"

Benjy was thrilled. He couldn't have wished for anything better. Rory looked at him enviously.

"You are jolly lucky!" he said.

"I *am!*" said Benjy, and he rubbed his hands in glee. What a treat to look forward to!

XIV

BENJY HAS A BIRTHDAY

When the others heard what Benjy's birthday treat from Tammylan was to be, they wished and wished that their birthdays were near too. Sheila and Penny had come back thrilled with their new dresses — but they forgot all about them when they heard the tale of the squirrels and their drey. Penny wanted to go off to the woods at once, and climb the tree.

"What! In your new frock!" cried Auntie Bess. "Certainly not, Penny. No climbing trees for *you*, please. Or for Sheila either. What's all this about spending the night with Tammylan, Benjy? You'll have to ask your uncle."

But he didn't need to, because Tammylan spoke to Uncle Tim one morning as he went round his fields. Uncle Tim was quite willing to listen. He agreed to let the boy spend the night with Tammylan. "But he must take a mackintosh sheet with him, to spread on the ground," said Uncle Tim. "It may be all right for you to live as you do — but the boy might take a chill. He's not used to it."

Benjy was overjoyed when Uncle Tim told him he had seen Tammylan and agreed to the birthday treat. He danced round the farmyard like a mad thing and the hens fled squawking to hide.

"Have pity on my hens, Benjy, for goodness' sake!" called Auntie Bess. "You'll frighten them out of their feathers!"

Benjy's birthday dawned fair and warm. The sun shone down hotly, and not even a wisp of cloud sailed over the sky. It was perfect birthday weather. Benjy was very happy.

He had lovely presents. Uncle Tim and Auntie Bess gave him boots and leggings just like Uncle Tim wore. How grand he felt when he put them on!

Sheila gave him a new book about animals. Rory gave him six tomato plants that he had bought at the market especially for Benjy. Benjy loved tomatoes — and now he could grow and pick his own!

"Thanks, Rory," said Benjy. "I shall take them out of their pots and plant them in that sunny spot by the wall where Aunt Bess said we could have a garden. And you and Sheila and Penny shall have the first three tomatoes! Golly, shan't I love picking my own tomatoes!"

Penny gave him a big tin of toffees that she had bought out of her own money. Taffy gave him a stick of his own that he had cut from the hedge for Benjy. That was a great surprise, and the boy was proud of his fine hazel stick.

His mother and father sent him some money to spend. He put it away safely in his purse. He didn't want anything at the moment, but it would be very useful when he did.

Uncle Tim took all the children in the pony-trap to market that morning. This was a treat they simply loved. It was good to see the fat cows, and to smell the rich market smell. It was fun to see the cackling geese, and to look at the grunting pigs in their pens. The market-women had golden butter to sell, and fresh brown eggs, bright green gooseberries, pots of homemade jam, greens from the garden, and many other things.

"Things feel *real*, somehow, out in the country," said Rory, staring round at everything, his eyes wandering off to the blue hills in the distance. "There's plenty of room, for one thing, and your eyes can look for miles. And there's the good animal, earthy smell — and everybody's doing something that matters — you know — milking cows, or selling eggs, or driving geese. I shall hate to go back to town!"

"Don't let's think about it!" said Benjy. "Come on — I shall spend some of my birthday money on ice-creams!"

At teatime there was an enormous cake covered with pink and white icing. On it was written in Auntie Bess's handwriting, "Many Happy Returns to Benjy". Eleven coloured candles stood proudly upright in sugar roses.

"This is the loveliest birthday I've ever had!" said Benjy, with a sigh of happiness. "Thank you, Aunt Bess, for making such a lovely cake. I usually have shop birthday cakes, and they aren't nearly so nice as this."

The cake was gorgeous, and each of the children managed two pieces. "I don't know what your mother would say if she saw you eating now," said Aunt Bess, looking at the fat, rosy faces round the table. "She told me you picked at your food, never asked for second helpings, and fussed over everything — so I thought I was going to have really difficult children!"

The children thought back to their London days. "Well, I never felt hungry," said Penny, remembering.

"And nothing ever tasted really nice to me," said Benjy. "I say, Aunt Bess — could I take a piece of my birthday cake to Tammylan? He'd be so pleased."

"Of course," said Auntie Bess. "Take him a nice big piece. He'll enjoy it — always eating those roots and toadstools and wild fruits! I wonder he keeps well!"

"He's awfully strong," said Benjy, munching at his cake. "He can climb a tree in a trice, and jump over the widest streams, and carry a fallen tree over his shoulder."

"Marvellous man!" said Uncle Tim. "Well — I suppose you'll soon be going off to spend the night with him? Got your mackintosh sheet out?"

"Yes," said Benjy. "But I wish I didn't have to take it. I'd like to feel the heather tickling me all night long!"

"I suppose we'll see you back to-morrow sometime," said Auntie Bess. "Well, you're a lucky boy — you've had a marvellous birthday, and, although most children's birthdays end when they go to bed, yours will still go on to-night!"

Benjy felt happy every time he thought of spending the night with Tammylan. He hugged himself in a funny way he had, and the others laughed at him.

"Mind you tell us *everything* when you come back," said Sheila. "Every single thing!"

"Of course," said Benjy, and he went to get his mackintosh sheet. It was in a tight little roll and he slung it over his shoulder on some string. He took a pocketful of the toffees that Penny had given him, and a big piece of his birthday cake wrapped up in paper. He had on his new boots and leggings, and in his hand was the stout hazel stick that Taffy had given him.

He felt very important and grand. Leggings made him feel manly. He wasn't very big for his age, but now he felt twice as old as he shouted good-bye to the others, and strode away down the lane, his stick swinging in his hand.

Benjy whistled as he went, and hoped he would meet the farm-men. He tucked his stick under his arm as he had seen his uncle do. Then he fished a toffee out of his pocket, and after that he couldn't whistle any more because the toffee took a lot of managing.

The sun was sending slanting rays between the trees as he came near to Tammylan's little growing house. The river shone gold, for it reflected the western sky. Blackbirds were fluting clearly, and a yellowhammer somewhere sang its monotonous little song. "Little bit of bread and no *cheese*! Little bit of bread and no *cheese*!"

Tammylan was waiting for him, sitting at the open doorway of his little green house. "Many happy returns!" he said to Benjy.

"Thanks," said Benjy. "I've had a fine birthday. See my new leggings?"

"Grand!" said Tammylan. "And that's a new stick, I see. Well — here's my present for you!"

He dropped a tiny bundle of warm fur into Benjy's hands. The boy gave a soft cry, and looked down.

"A baby squirrel!" he said. "Oh, how lovely! Where did you get it?"

"It's one I've been keeping for you," said Tammylan. "The mother was accidentally killed — caught in a trap, poor thing — and of her three babies, two died. But this one was still alive in the nest when I found it. So I brought it here and fed it — and kept it for your birthday. It will be like a little dog, always with you, always at your call."

"Oh, Tammylan, I couldn't want a better present!" said Benjy, really overjoyed. He had never in his life had a pet — and now here was the quaintest, softest ball of fur, ready to become his faithful little friend. It should live on his shoulder! It should come at his call. What should he call it?

"Shall I call it Scamper?" he asked Tammylan. "Squirrels scamper over the ground and up the trees so quickly. And I could call it Scamp for short, if it's a rascal of a squirrel."

"Good idea," said Tammylan. "Now, Scamper, cuddle down for a while in your new master's arms. We want to watch the sun go down. There will be a marvellous sunset to-night."

Scamper had already cuddled into the crook of Benjy's right arm. Its bright black eyes closed. Its little furry tail coiled round its nose. It was asleep.

Benjy sat hugging his new pet, feeling its tiny heart beating quickly against his arm. He leaned against one side of the doorway and Tammylan sat against the other side. The tree-house had grown leaves to such an extent that they made a completely green roof, and hung down the sides.

Benjy peeped inside the house. To his great delight he saw that Tammylan had made up another bed, opposite to his. Dried moss and heather were banked up, and an old rug was thrown at the end.

"I can see my bed!" said the boy. "Isn't it a pity — I've got to have this silly mackintosh sheet to lie on. It will spoil the feel of the heather."

"No, it won't," said Tammylan. "We'll put it on the ground, *beneath* the heather — and pile the bedding on top! Then you won't get the damp striking up from the ground — and you'll still lie on the heather and moss!"

"Oh, good!" said Benjy, pleased. His squirrel stirred in his arms and he stroked its back gently. The little thing stretched itself and fell asleep again.

"And now let us be quiet, for I am expecting a visitor to-night," said Tammylan. "When you hear his whistle keep quite still."

"*Whistle!*" said Benjy, amazed. "Is it a man, then?"

"Oh no," said Tammylan.

"But no animal whistles," said Benjy. "Oh, you mean a bird?"

"Not even a bird!" said Tammylan. "Now, be quiet, and wait."

XV

A NIGHT IN THE TREE-HOUSE

Benjy sat perfectly still, the baby squirrel asleep on his knee. The sun sank lower, and the sky became pink and gold. The quiet backwater of the river reflected the sky, and Benjy was almost dazzled as he looked at it. A buttercup field across the river shone and glowed in the last rays of the sun — and then the big round disc sank half-way over the sky-line.

The light went out of the buttercups. The clouds faded from pink to grey. Two bars of gold remained in the sky — and then, just as Benjy was watching them fade to a pale blue, he heard the whistle.

It was clear as a flute, and it came echoing over the water. There was something bird-like in it, and yet it wasn't a bird Benjy felt sure. It came again, fluting over the water, clear and lovely.

Tammylan answered the whistle. He sent out a call so exactly like the whistle that Benjy had to look at him to make sure it came from him. Tammylan nodded towards the water. "Here he comes," he said.

Benjy looked eagerly at the darkening water. He saw, coming gradually towards them, a dark blunt head just on the surface. The body belonging to the head was swimming below. Benjy couldn't make out what it was at all.

With hardly a ripple to show that anyone was swimming there, the creature moved towards the bank. It clambered out — and Benjy saw that it was a big dark-brown animal, with a long tail and strong webbed feet.

"An otter!" he said. "Oh, Tammylan!"

Tammylan whistled to the otter again and it shook itself and came towards him, moving easily over the ground. Its small, bright eyes looked at him, and then at Benjy.

"All right, friend, you are safe with Benjy," said Tammylan, in his special voice — the one he always used for animals and birds. The otter moved closer to him and lay down, its head on Tammylan's leg. Tammylan ran his fingers over the otter's small, rounded ears.

"Have you had good hunting, friend?" he said. "Have you eaten fish to-day? Did you catch them by swimming below them, and darting upwards more quickly than they could swim? Did you turn over the river stones and hunt for the crayfish you love? Did you find the frogs and skin them for a meal?"

The otter made a snickering noise, and moved its head a little higher up Tammylan's leg. Benjy watched enviously, wishing that the otter would come to him too.

"Feel him, Benjy," said Tammylan. "Feel his thick fur. He has two coats of hair — one a thick, short undercoat to protect his body from the water, and the other a coat of much longer hairs. You can feel them growing out of his short coat."

Benjy felt them. "Doesn't he ever get cold and wet, swimming like that?" he asked.

"No," said Tammylan. "His body never gets wet. He is a marvellous swimmer, Benjy, as graceful as any fish."

"What does he do when he swims under the water?" asked Benjy. "Doesn't the water get into his ears?"

"No. He closes both his ears then," said Tammylan. "See his thick, strong tail, Benjy. He uses it as a rudder in the water. He is a beautiful beast in the river, and when he gambols there for fun he is a joy to watch."

"I saw that he had webbed feet," said Benjy. "They help him to swim fast, of course. What a lovely whistle he has!"

"Yes," said Tammylan. "I hear it often at night now, coming down the river. The night-sounds are lovely to hear — the bark of a distant fox — the whistle of the otter — the hoot of the owl. This friend of mine visits me often at night, and sometimes, if he is near, he comes in answer to my whistle."

"How did you first know him?" asked Benjy. "He is so tame!"

"Three years ago his father and mother made a nesting-place in a hole among the alder roots, a little way down this backwater," said Tammylan. "It was a good hole, with an entrance below the water and one above it on the bank at the back. In this hole the otters brought up three cubs — fur-covered youngsters eager to learn to swim and hunt fish."

"Eager to *learn*?" asked Benjy. "Did they have to be taught, then? Didn't they know it without being taught, as birds know how to build nests, and ducks know how to swim?"

"No — the young otters had to be taught, Benjy," said Tammylan. "I used to hide in the bushes and watch the parents take the three cubs into the water and teach them the business of hunting. They could not stay under the water for very long at first without breathing — but they soon learnt that trick. Then they learnt to chase the fish and swim below them. They were taught to bring their catch to the bank and eat it there — but to leave the tail! It is not good manners in the otter family to eat the tail of a fish."

Benjy laughed, and the little squirrel stirred, settled itself again and slept. The otter looked at Benjy with glittering eyes. Tammylan ran his fingers down its neck, and it snickered and rolled against him.

"Well," said Tammylan, "the otter hounds came to hunt the otters one day. The parents fled away, swimming for dear life. The dogs caught two of the cubs — they killed them. And then this one, who was the third cub, tried to make its way to a hiding-place across the river, unseen. But the hounds saw the slight ripple he made — and two of them caught him. They bit his back legs cruelly. He fought hard, and they let him go."

"Poor little cub," said Benjy. "I wish things needn't be so cruel to one another."

"The cub managed to crawl back to his old nesting-hole," said Tammylan. "And there I found him after the hunt was over. He crawled to me out of the back entrance,

and I brought him here and looked after him till his legs were better and he could swim again. That is how he and I became friends."

"It's a fine story," said Benjy. "Penny would cry over that, I know. She can't bear anything to be hurt."

"This otter has travelled far in the winter days," said Tammylan. "He wandered over the land at night, for he is a good traveller. But now he lives in the river, and knows every inch of it from the source to the mouth!"

Benjy sat quiet, thinking over the story of the otter, wondering where the parents had gone. What a good thing Tammylan had been about at the time of the hunt! How many creatures had he healed and saved? Benjy was proud to have him for a friend.

The moon rose up, and the river changed from black to silver. Pools of cold moonlight lay on the ground. Rabbits came out everywhere. Owls hooted weirdly, and once there came such a screech that Benjy jumped violently and awoke the squirrel.

"Whatever's that?" asked the boy.

"A barn-owl across the water," said Tammylan. "They always screech like that. Now Benjy — what about some supper — and then bed?"

"I could stay here for hours," said Benjy, with a sigh. "Doesn't the world seem strange and unreal by moonlight, Tammylan? Oh — I nearly forgot — I've got some of my birthday cake for you!"

The boy gave the slice to Tammylan. He was very pleased, and ate it as he sat, giving a few crumbs to the otter at his feet. Then he lit a small fire and cooked the boy a strange but delicious meal. They ate it in the moonlight, and then drank something that Tammylan called Nettle-gingerbeer. It was made of nettle leaves and tasted queer but cool and sweet.

"And now for bed!" said Tammylan. "I bathe in the morning, Benjy. Will that suit you? We will take a plunge in the river then. Take off your coat and shorts and I'll roll you up in the rug."

The mackintosh sheet was laid flat on the ground under Benjy's bed of heather and moss. When he was ready Tammylan rolled him up in the rug, and then the boy cuddled down on his heather bed. It felt soft and springy, though a few sprigs stuck into him here and there. Benjy arranged them comfortably, and then let himself sink down into the queer bed. It smelt nice. The squirrel curled up on his tummy, still sleeping.

"Where's the otter going to?" asked Benjy sleepily. "Is it going back to the river?"

"I think he wants to sleep here for the night," said Tammylan. "Do you mind? He sometimes likes company, you see."

"Do I *mind!*" said Benjy. "Why, I'd love it! I never, never thought I'd go to sleep with a squirrel on top of me, a wild man near me, and an otter at our feet!"

Benjy didn't want to go to sleep at all. He wanted to stay awake and feel the strange delight of the little growing house, the breathing of the otter, the warmth of the squirrel — he wanted to lie and look at the moon which was now shining straight into the open doorway of the house. He wished he could hear the owls all night long — and the plash-plash-plash of the water nearby, and the whispering in the trees above.

But his eyes wouldn't stay open. They closed and he slept as peacefully as Tammylan, the otter, and the tiny furry squirrel.

XVI

TWO MORE FRIENDS

Benjy awoke first in the morning, because the squirrel was trying to sit on his nose. Benjy couldn't think what was happening. His eyes shot open, he gasped for breath — and sat up. The squirrel fell off and leapt to the ground. Benjy picked it up at once — he didn't want it to scamper out of the doorway and be lost!

The otter was gone. Tammylan lay on his side, sleeping peacefully. Faint daylight shone into the open doorway. The splash of the water against the bank sounded like a little tune — plishy-plash-plash, plishy-plash-plash.

"I wonder if the sun is rising yet," thought Benjy, lying on his back and looking up into the greenness of the roof. "Oh, isn't it lovely to wake up like this, in a wood by the water! I shan't wake Tammylan. I shall just enjoy it all quite by myself — with my squirrel!"

The squirrel had curled up on a warm part of Benjy's neck, and was now asleep again.

A few birds began to sing. The light grew stronger. A breeze got up and made the trees say "Sh! Sh! Sh!" to one another — at least, that is what Benjy thought it sounded like.

Then a small animal appeared in the doorway, and stood up on its hind legs, sniffing gently. It was quite surprised to see Benjy looking at it. Benjy moved his squirrel and sat up, leaning on an elbow to watch the newcomer.

"I think it's a rat," thought Benjy. "I don't like rats. I really don't. They are about the only animal I don't want to be friends with."

He watched the furry creature as it ran quickly to Tammylan's couch. It put one paw on the wild man's bed and stood there, waiting to see if Tammylan would move or speak.

But Tammylan slept on. The little creature scratched itself behind the ears, and seemed to think a little. Then it made up its mind that its friend was asleep—and it ran to the doorway. Benjy made up *his* mind to see where it went.

So he cautiously got up and went to the open doorway. The furry animal had run to the river bank. Benjy followed. The little creature did not seem to mind him in the least. It slipped down to a small ledge, near the water, and began to nibble at some juicy horsetail stems. Every now and again it looked up at Benjy as if to say, "Try a bit! It's good!"

There was a noise behind Benjy, and he looked round. It was Tammylan. He had awakened, missed Benjy, and had come to look for him. He saw him at once, by the river.

"Hallo, Tammylan," said Benjy eagerly. "I did love waking up in your tree-house! Look—do you see that rat down there? It came to visit you—but you were fast asleep. I don't think I want a rat for a friend. *Is* he your friend?"

"That little creature down there is a great friend of mine," said Tammylan, squatting down on the bank beside Benjy. "But he is no rat!"

"I thought he was!" said Benjy. "I know lots of people who would have killed him if they could—everyone seems to hate rats."

"Yes—rats have a bad name, and they certainly deserve it," said Tammylan. "But this poor little animal should not be made to suffer because he happens to be just a little like a rat to look at!"

"What is he, then?" asked Benjy in surprise.

"He is a water-vole," said Tammylan. "A quiet and harmless little animal, who loves the water and only wants to live at peace. But as soon as anyone sees him they cry, 'A rat! A rat!' and throw stones at him to kill him. Watch him as he nibbles that stem—he is a dear little thing, harming nothing and no one!"

The water-vole looked up at Tammylan. It sprang up the bank and ran on to Tammylan's knee. The wild man stroked the long glossy fur. It was a rich reddish-brown with grey hairs here and there. Tammylan rolled the vole over to tickle him and showed Benjy the yellow-grey fur below.

"He is not *really* like a rat," said Tammylan. "Look at his head—it is thicker and shorter than a rat's—and see his rounded muzzle. You know that the rat has a pointed one, don't you? And look at the vole's hairy tail—not nearly so long as the rat's bare, scaly one."

"Yes—now you say all these things, I can see that the vole isn't like a rat," said Benjy, stroking the tiny head with its round ears. "What a shame that it is killed in mistake for a rat! You say it's a *water*-vole, Tammylan. Can it swim, then?"

"Watch and see," said Tammylan. He set the vole down gently on the bank and gave it a little push. The vole at once leapt down to the water and entered it with a little plop. "When you walk along the river bank and hear that 'plop' you will know that a water-vole has seen you and gone home!" said Tammylan.

"Where does he live?" asked Benjy, trying to see whereabouts in the water the vole was. But he could see nothing.

"He has a cosy hidey-hole in the bank over there," said Tammylan, pointing to where reeds grew thickly. "The entrance is under the water—but, like the otter, our vole has a back entrance above ground. Come and watch him peep out of it."

They got up and went to the reeds. Tammylan parted them and showed Benjy a small hole. He pursed up his lips and made a curious sucking noise. At once the rounded furry head of the water-vole appeared, and two black eyes looked up inquiringly at Tammylan.

"All right, old fellow," said Tammylan. "We just wanted to see you at your back-door! He swam to his underwater entrance, Benjy, ran up his burrow — and, when he heard my call, popped up to see us."

The water-vole popped back and disappeared. "Does he sleep all the winter?" asked Benjy as they went back to the tree-house.

"Oh no," said Tammylan. "He comes to see me during the darkest days of winter. He sometimes lays up a little store of food for himself — and in the New Year I have seen him chewing the tender willow shoots. He has two little cousins you must look out for, Benjy — the small field-vole, which we often call the short-tailed field-mouse, and the little bank-vole. Now — what about a bathe?"

The sun was shining warmly now. The river looked cool and inviting. It wasn't long before Benjy and Tammylan were having a fine time in the water, splashing one another and shouting. Tammylan could swim like an otter. Benjy wished he could do the same — but he couldn't!

They dressed, and Tammylan cooked a queer but delicious breakfast. The tiny squirrel sat on Benjy's shoulder all the time. Tammylan picked some tender shoots for it, and it held one in its hands and nibbled it.

"I do love Scamper," said Benjy, rubbing his head against the furry mite. "Do you think he will be happy with me?"

"He will soon run off into the woods if he isn't!" said Tammylan. "I will show you what shoots to feed him on. Later on he will love acorns and nuts. I will tell you the toadstools he likes, too."

"I *have* had a lovely time," sighed Benjy, looking round at the tree-house, the river, and the sunny freckles on the ground. "I wish I could stay here always."

"I would like you to," said Tammylan. "It is not many boys who have the feeling for the wild creatures that you have — but you belong to your family — and it is time you went back to them, Benjy. They will be wondering what you are doing."

"Yes — I must go back, I have my jobs to do," said Benjy, standing up. "I'll come and see you soon again, Tammylan — and thanks for a lovely time — and a lovely pet! I'll bring Scamper to see you whenever I come."

"I'll come with you a little way," said Tammylan. "It's such a lovely morning."

The man and the boy walked together through the green woods. They came to where bushes of yellow broom were waving in the summer breeze. As they passed near them a tiny creature ran across their path. They stopped, and Benjy pointed to where it ran.

"What's that?" he cried. "A mouse? Isn't it small!"

"That was a tiny harvest-mouse," said Tammylan. "Almost the smallest of all our animals! Let us look in this broom bush . . . it ran there. Perhaps it has its nest there. We could see it."

Tammylan looked into the bush. He made a funny chirping noise, rather like a bird. Benjy listened in astonishment when he heard someone chirping back! Surely a mouse didn't chirp!

But the harvest-mouse apparently did — for Tammylan

114

beckoned to Benjy, and showed him the nest. It was really marvellous. It was built among the stems of the broom, about seven or eight inches from the ground. The mouse had cleverly used some of the stiff stems to hold up her nest, which she had made in the shape of a little ball. It was made of split blades of grass, very neatly plaited together to make a cosy, strong nest.

"It's the best nest I ever saw in my life," said Benjy, full of wonder. "I couldn't make such a beauty myself! Where's the entrance?"

"Oh, just anywhere!" said Tammylan, and he showed Benjy how he could force an opening in any place, between the woven grass. "There is a family of six or seven inside, I should think – and the mother too!"

"But how can they all get into that three-inch nest!" said Benjy. Tammylan gently forced a space in the outside of the nest and Benjy caught a glimpse of a closely packed family, small and frightened.

"We won't disturb them any more," said Tammylan. "It is only because the mother heard me chirping to her that she knows I am friendly. Listen – she will chirp back again!"

Tammylan chirped loudly – and from the nest the little harvest-mouse answered with a softer chirp. Benjy tried the chirp, too – but it was not so easy as it sounded!

"Another noise to practise!" thought Benjy. "The snake noise – the otter whistle – goodness, I shall be a walking menagerie of noises soon!"

"Watch for the little harvest-mouse as you go about the fields this summer," said Tammylan. "Especially in the cornfields, Benjy. The mouse is so small that it can climb up a stalk of corn, hold on by its tail, and nibble the grain! It is really a pretty sight to see, with its thick, yellow-red fur, blunt little nose, and bright black eyes."

They came to the stile and Tammylan swung off up the hill, and called good-bye. Benjy went back to the farm with Scamper on his shoulder.

The others came running to meet him.

"What did you do? Did you sleep in the tree-house?" cried Penny.

"What's that on your shoulder!" called Rory.

"It's a baby squirrel!" squealed Sheila. "Oh, where did you get it from, Benjy?"

"It was my birthday present from Tammylan," said Benjy proudly. "Aren't I lucky?"

The squirrel looked at the three children with bright black eyes. It did not seem in the least frightened. It lay against Benjy's neck as the boy told all about his adventures of the night before.

"Oh! Fancy sleeping with a squirrel and an otter!" said Penny, her eyes as wide as the squirrel's. "Oh, you are the luckiest boy in all the world."

"Yes, I am!" said Benjy, patting Scamper. And he really meant it!

XVII

THE TAIL THAT BROKE OFF

The little squirrel was very happy with the children. They made a fuss of it, fed it with all kinds of dainties, as well as the food that Tammylan had told Benjy to give it, and it became as much a pet as Shadow, the collie.

It usually lived on Benjy's shoulder, and it always slept on his bed. It leapt here and there, bounded up the curtains and down, and gave Auntie Bess a hundred shocks a day. But she liked the pretty little thing, and was only afraid that the cat might catch it.

"I think Tammylan would like to see how Scamper has grown," said Benjy one fine sunny day. "Let's go and see him, and take the squirrel with us."

"Take your tea with you and have a picnic," said Auntie Bess.

"Oh yes—let's take our tea!" cried Penny, who was always ready for a picnic. So Aunt Bess packed up tomato sandwiches, egg sandwiches, ginger buns, and milk, and they set off for their picnic.

They went first to Tammylan's cave and then to the tree-house but Tammylan was not to be found. So they decided he must have gone on one of his explorations, or to visit one of his friends, and they chose a nice sunny place in the heather for their tea. Scamper nibbled at the tomato sandwiches in delight, but he couldn't bear the taste of the ginger buns. He scolded Sheila for giving him a bit, and stamped his little feet hard on Benjy's shoulder.

"Oh, what a naughty temper you've got!" laughed Sheila. Then she suddenly gave a squeal, and pointed to something that lay basking in the sun nearby.

"Look!" she said. "A snake!"

They all looked. They saw a creature about eighteen inches long. Its head was small and short, and the tail tapered gradually to a point. It was covered with scales. The bright eyes gleamed in its head.

"Well — but what *sort* of a snake!" said Benjy in wonder. "It isn't a viper, that's quite certain. And it isn't a grass snake, because its body is so different — and I'm sure it isn't a smooth snake. Tammylan said there were only three snakes in this country — and he must be wrong!"

"I wonder if it bites," said Sheila, not at all sure that she liked the look of it.

"No, I shouldn't think so," said Benjy. "Tammylan did say very clearly that we only have one poisonous snake here — and this one is most certainly not the viper!"

"Catch it, Benjy," said Rory. "Then we can show it to Tammylan. We can tell him he's wrong — there's a fourth kind of snake in our country!"

"Well — I can't think Tammylan is wrong," said Benjy, puzzled. "But I really must find out about this. Hold Scamper, Rory. I'll see if I can catch the snake. Keep quiet, all of you!"

Benjy crept quietly over the heather. The creature did not seem to hear him coming. It was enjoying the sunshine, and lay there, its long body stretched out to the warm rays.

Benjy got very close — closer — and then he made a grab at the snake. In a trice it wriggled through his fingers — but Benjy had hold of it by the tail!

"Got you!" he cried.

But had he? What was this? The frightened creature wriggled away in the heather, and left behind in Benjy's hand—a tail! It jumped about in a most peculiar manner.

"I say! Just look at that!" said Benjy, in the greatest astonishment.

"Oh, Benjy! How cruel of you! You've broken its tail off!" said Penny, almost in tears.

"I *didn't*!" said Benjy indignantly. "I just held it, to catch it—and its tail broke off in my hand. You saw it! Do you suppose it did it on purpose, to get away?"

"Lizards do that, but not snakes," said Rory, staring at the jerking tail-end in Benjy's hand. "I wish Tammylan was here. He would be sure to know about this."

Scamper sniffed at the tail-end and then jumped on to Benjy's shoulder in disgust. He didn't like the look of the

tail at all. Neither did anyone, really. Benjy put it away in his pocket and tried to forget about it.

But although they went on with their picnic, nobody felt really hungry now. Somehow it seemed spoilt. They couldn't help wondering if the creature had been hurt — and Benjy felt really very guilty. Suppose Tammylan called him cruel and was angry with him?

Just as they were finishing they saw Tammylan in the distance. Rory got up and waved to him. He came over to the children, smiling.

"Tammylan, does it hurt a snake to have its tail broken off?" asked Penny as soon as he came near.

"Whatever do you mean?" asked Tammylan in surprise. "A snake never breaks its tail off."

"But it *does*!" said poor Benjy; and, very red in the face, he pulled the tail-end out of his pocket.

Tammylan looked at the tail, and then he looked at Benjy's guilty face. Then, to the children's surprise and relief, he began to laugh.

"Oh dear!" he said at last. "So you really thought you'd been strong enough to pull a snake's tail off. No — that's not a snake's tail."

"But it *is*, Tammylan," cried all the children. "It is, it is!"

"Listen!" said Tammylan. "I told you we only had three kinds of snakes in our country, didn't I? Well, this isn't one of them. It belongs to the lizard family, not to the snakes. It is a slow-worm, or, to give it another of its silly names, a blind-worm."

"Oh!" said the children. Benjy blushed. "I ought to have known," he said. "I've read about it in my books."

"Now, what about looking more closely at a slow-worm?" said Tammylan. "Not the one who made you a present of his tail, Benjy—he won't appear again to-day! But I dare say we shall see another, if we search about a bit."

The children watched Tammylan as he quietly hunted on the sandy banks for another slow-worm. At last he spied one. The children watched him in excitement.

"I guess this one will break off its tail too!" whispered Rory. But it didn't. No—Tammylan knew how to catch slow-worms! He caught it just behind the head, not by the tail, and brought it over to the children.

The slow-worm did not seem in the least frightened. That was the strange part about the wild man. No animal or bird ever showed fright when he spoke to it or touched it. The slow-worm lay in his hands, and even when Tammylan no longer held it by the back of the neck it did not glide away.

"Here is our slow-worm," said Tammylan. "I am afraid that far too many people make the same mistake as you did, children, and think it is a snake! So the poor old harmless slow-worm is killed by any passer-by. It can't sting. It can't bite. It eats worms, slugs, and insects, and does no harm to anyone! If only people would learn a little more about our wild creatures, no slow-worm would ever be killed."

"Why is it called a *slow*-worm?" asked Rory. "You know, the one that wriggled away from Benjy wasn't slow—it was a quick-worm!"

Tammylan laughed. "I will tell you the three names that foolish people have given to this legless lizard," he said. "One is slow-worm—but, as you said, it *isn't* slow. Another name is blind-worm—but, as you see, it re-markably bright eyes—and please notice the eyelids, which a snake never has! The third name, even sillier, is deaf-adder. It isn't deaf, and it certainly isn't an adder!"

The slow-worm put out its tongue and Benjy gave an exclamation. "Look! Its tongue isn't forked like a snake's."

"No," said Tammylan. "It is only notched. I am glad you noticed that, Benjy. Good boy!"

"But, Tammylan, why did the slow-worm break off its tail?" asked Benjy. "Will it grow again?"

"It broke its tail off because it knew it could escape that way," said Tammylan. "A snake cannot do that, of course! Yes—it will grow again, though it may not be quite so nicely fitting a tail as before! Look, children—do you see that slow-worm over there? It has just come out on the bank. Look at its tail—at some time or other it has been broken off. Do you see where the new one began to grow again, at the break?"

"Oh yes!" said Sheila. "I can see it quite easily! Well I *am* glad we didn't hurt the slow-worm, Tammylan. I do hope it will soon grow a very nice new tail."

"It will take it a little time," said the wild man. "But it will grow it all right! And what is more, it would grow a third one if it had to!"

Tammylan let the slow-worm he was holding slip to the ground. It wriggled away like a flash and disappeared. "A *quick*-worm, as you said, Rory!" said Tammylan. "Yet it isn't a worm either. It *does* suffer from a lot of stupid names, doesn't it! I wish you could see its young ones, later on in the summer. They are amusing little things. Last year I kept a whole family of them."

"What were they like?" asked Benjy.

"Oh—like wriggling silver needles!" said Tammylan. "They were perfectly lovely, and I didn't need to feed them myself at all. They could catch their own food even when they were not much bigger than a darning-needle!"

"Do you know where any lizards are?" asked Benjy.

"Good gracious, yes!" said Tammylan. "I can call any amount of lizards for you! Would you like me to?"

"Oh *yes!*" cried everyone in delight. "Call them — and we'll watch them come!"

Tammylan got up. He led the way to a sheltered part of the hillside. Heather grew all around, and the scent of gorse came warmly on the breeze. Tammylan pointed to a small patch of warm sand.

"Watch that patch," he said. "I'm going to whistle."

He whistled — a curious low whistle, on one or two notes. On and on and on went the strange whistle, till it seemed part of the breeze and the rustling of a nearby birch tree. The children watched and waited, thrilled.

And then, from out of their hiding-places came the little lizards! First one came running, a little thing about five inches long. With its tiny fingers and toes it ran over the heather and went to the sandy patch. It stood there, slightly raised on its two front arms, its head on one side as if it were listening — as indeed it was.

"Isn't it sweet!" whispered Penny. "Look how it winks at Tammylan!"

It really did seem as if it were winking, for it flashed its eyelids up and down over its bright eyes. Then another lizard ran out with a gliding motion, and it too stopped suddenly and listened.

"They run as if they are clockwork," said Benjy. "Oh, here's another — and another!"

Soon the patch of hot sand was full of listening lizards — at least, they all *looked* as if they were listening! Tammylan stopped his whistling, and the lizards began to play about, rushing from one place to another, just as if their clockwork started and stopped very suddenly! They were fun to watch.

"That lizard's got a very peculiar tail," said Benjy. "The one at the edge of the sand."

"He has broken it off, just as the slow-worm did," said Tammylan. "But it hasn't mended very well — it is rather rough and ready! The new one doesn't seem to fit."

The lizards ran at any insect that appeared. The children were near enough to see their notched tongues, and to marvel at the tiny, delicate fingers and toes they had.

"I do wish I could hold one," said Benjy. "I'd like to feel those little fingers and toes on my hand."

"I'll catch one for you," said Tammylan. He slid his hand quietly along, and then made a firm grab at the nearest lizard. He caught it behind the shoulders and put it on his other hand.

"It's no use making your little body go all stiff like that!" said Tammylan to the lizard. "I am not going to allow you to break off your tail!"

The lizard soon recovered from its fright and lay quietly on Tammylan's hand. He whistled softly to it and it listened, its eyes blinking every now and again. Then Tammylan put it gently on to Benjy's hand and the boy felt the touch of the tiny fingers and toes. It was lovely. Scamper, the squirrel, who had been on Benjy's shoulder all the time, did not at all like to see the lizard in Benjy's hand. He suddenly ran down Benjy's arm and made a grab at the lizard.

But in a trice the little thing was off and away, hidden in the heather.

"Oh, jealous little Scamper!" said Tammylan. "Look, Benjy, more lizards have come out again. Do you see that one climbing up the heather-stalk? See its pretty underside of bright orange?"

"Oh yes!" said Benjy. "I do like the lizards, Tammylan. I wish I had one for a pet."

"I had one two years ago," said Tammylan. "It made itself very useful to me, for it lived in my cave and ate all the flies that bothered me! But when the winter came it went away to sleep."

"I suppose there was no insect food for it in the winter-time," said Penny, wisely. "So it *had* to go to sleep."

"Quite right, Penny," said Tammylan. "Well now, I must go. I have to get something to eat, for I've had nothing to-day so far. I must hunt for the things I like best!"

Tammylan stood up. Rory looked at his watch. "We must go too," he said. "Well, good hunting, Tammylan — and a fine meal when you've finished!"

XVIII

THE STRANGE FROG-RAIN

One morning the children were sent to another farm with a message from Uncle Tim. It was fine when they set out, but on the way back a great purple cloud blew up and covered the whole of the sky.

"Gracious! What's going to happen!" cried Sheila, half afraid. "Is it a storm coming, do you think?"

As she spoke, there came the roll of thunder some distance away. A few large drops of rain pattered down. Then more and more, like big silver pennies. They struck the children quite hard.

"It feels as if someone up in the sky is *throwing* rain-drops at us," said Penny. "Goodness, I *am* getting wet!"

Then the rain came down properly, in long silver lines, slanting over the fields and woods. The thunder rolled again, but was not very near. Penny didn't like it. She was afraid of storms.

She began to cry. "What shall we do? We mustn't shelter under trees in a thunderstorm because it's dangerous—but, oh Rory, I shall get so wet! I've only got this little thin frock on."

Rory stood still and looked round. "I believe we can't be very far from Tammylan's cave," he said. "I don't know this way very well, but I believe if we go down that lane, cut across that field, and go over that patch of heather, we'll come to the cave from the opposite side. Come on—run down the lane!"

The children began to run—but before they had gone very far they slowed down in surprise. The lane was absolutely full of small frogs! They covered the road, they hopped from the ditches, they made the wayside quite dark with their hopping bodies!

"Look, look!" shouted Rory. "Did you ever see so many frogs?"

A lady came by on a bicycle. She too was astonished, and tried her best to ride without squashing the crowd of little frogs.

"It's frog-rain!" she called to the children. "It's raining frogs! That's where they're coming from!"

The children stared at her in astonishment, forgetting the rainstorm. They looked up into the sky to see if they could spy frogs coming down—but the rain was too hard for them to keep their heads up—and all the time more and more frogs filled the road till it really seemed as if they must be falling with the rain.

"It's most extraordinary!" said Benjy, gulping down some raindrops. "The frogs can't *really* come from the sky! How would they get up there? And yet there are thousands!"

"Of course they're coming down with the rain!" said Penny. "Why, look—plop, plop, hop, hop, you can almost seem them coming down with the raindrops!"

The lane was moving with frogs. They hopped around the children's feet, and it was very difficult to go through them without hurting them. At last they got to the end of the lane and set off across the field. The thunder was nearer now, and Penny began to cry again.

There were frogs in the field too, hundreds of them, though they could not be seen quite so clearly as on the road. Rory took Penny's hand and helped her along, for she could not run so quickly as the others. Benjy had got Scamper, the squirrel, tucked safely away in his pocket. Scamper hated the rain.

At last they came to the cave—and Tammylan was there! "My goodness, what drowned little rats!" he cried. "Come in—there's going to be a marvellous storm. I'm glad you were sensible enough not to shelter under a tree. Ah—

there's the lightning. Did you see it tear that dark cloud in half?"

"Do you like storms, then, Tammylan?" asked Penny in surprise.

"I love them," said Tammylan. "Grand things! The roll and crash of thunder, the sharpness of the lightning, the sting of the rain! Don't tell me you are afraid of a storm, Penny?"

"Well, you see," said Penny, "I once had a nurse who went and hid herself in a cupboard when there was a storm, so I thought it must be something very dreadful, and I always feel afraid too."

"And now here is someone who loves a storm and thinks it's one of the loveliest sights in the world, so you will be able to think differently!" said Tammylan, taking the little girl on his knee. "Goodness, how wet you are! Let's take off this thin little frock and wrap you in one of my rugs."

So, wrapped in a rug, Penny sat at the cave entrance to watch the storm. And because Tammylan loved it and was not in the least frightened, Penny saw the beauty of it too.

"Long, long ago men thought that the thunder was the noise made by great wooden balls rolled over the floor of heaven," said Tammylan. "Listen to the next rumble, Penny, and tell me if you think it sounds like that!"

The thunder obligingly rolled round the hills and the children laughed. "Yes — it's exactly like big wooden balls rolling over a great floor!" said Benjy. "Isn't it, Penny?"

Penny suddenly remembered the frogs. "Oh, Tammylan," she said, "whatever do you think happened as we came running here? It rained frogs all around us!"

"It couldn't do that," said Tammylan. "Rain is only rain."

"But, Tammylan, it really *was* raining frogs!" said

129

Penny. "I saw them plopping down all round me — thousands and thousands of them! And a lady on a bicycle told us it was raining frogs, too."

"Well, Penny, her eyes must have deceived her just as much as yours deceived *you!*" said Tammylan with a laugh. "Your own common sense will tell you that frogs do not live in the sky, and so they can't drop from there! You know where frogs come from, don't you?"

"From tadpoles," said Penny.

"Yes, and where do tadpoles live?" asked Tammylan. "In the clouds?"

"No, of course not — in the ponds," said Penny, beginning to feel rather silly.

"What do the others think about it?" said Tammylan, turning to them. "Did any of *you* think you saw frogs flying gracefully through the air, each riding on a silver raindrop?"

The children laughed — but they were puzzled all the same.

"No, Tammylan, none of us actually *saw* the frogs in the air," said Benjy honestly. "It only seemed very queer to see them in such thousands on the ground when the rain began. They weren't there before, I know."

"Quite right, Benjy," said Tammylan. "Well, there is a very simple explanation of the curious sight you saw. I'll tell you. You know that the frog spawn turned into tadpoles, and the tadpoles grew into small frogs, don't you?"

"Yes," said everyone.

"Well," said Tammylan, "there comes a time when all those thousands and thousands of small new frogs need to leave the pond and find somewhere else — a nice moist place in a ditch, perhaps, or in long meadow grass, where they may catch flies and grubs for their food. Now, no frog will leave the wet cool pond on a dry sunny day, for all frogs need moisture when they travel. So what happens? They wait until a terrific downpour of rain comes along — and then the same idea pops into the head of each restless frog!"

"And they all climb out of the pond and go travelling!" cried Benjy. "Of course! And that's how we saw so many all at once. It was their travelling time!"

"Yes," said the wild man. "They had left their home pond, where they had been born, and were hopping away to find a new home for themselves on land. And there they will stay, in ditches and moist places, all the summer through, feasting on flies and grubs, growing large and fat until the autumn — when they will once more return to their pond to sleep."

"And we thought it was raining frogs!" said Rory. "What stupids we are!"

"You are, rather," said Tammylan. "Never believe stupid things without first making quite sure they are right! This idea of frog-rain comes up every year — but if everyone really thought hard about it they would know there couldn't possibly be such a thing."

"There are plenty of frogs outside your cave, Tammylan," said Penny, watching them. "They are nearly all small ones, though. Where are the big ones?"

"Oh, the big ones have left the water some time ago," said Tammylan. "Those that you see are this year's crop of frogs! It takes a frog five years to grow up, you know. But some, if not most, of the creatures you saw in the lane must have been toads, not frogs, I should think. Look — there are some tiny toads over there, in a little batch together."

"They look exactly like frogs to me," said Rory. "I

131

don't know the difference!"

"Oh, Rory!" said Tammylan, pretending to be quite shocked. "Aren't you ashamed of knowing so little!"

Rory grinned. "Not a bit," he said, "when I've got someone like you to explain things to me!"

"Well, it's easy to show you the difference between a frog and a toad!" said Tammylan. He went out into the rain, which was now not nearly so bad, and fetched a frog. Then he did such a funny thing. He put his finger into his mouth, slightly blew out his cheeks, made a kind of humming noise, and jiggled his finger quickly from side to side of his mouth.

"Why, Tammylan, what are you . . ." began Penny in surprise. And then she stopped. For *someone* had heard the queer call! And that someone was a large old toad. He was under a big mossy stone just outside the cave. He came crawling out, and made his way to Tammylan.

"A very old friend of mine," said Tammylan, smiling round at the astonished children. "I won't tell you how old he is, for you wouldn't believe me. Would they, Bufo?"

Bufo, the toad, looked up at Tammylan out of coppery eyes. Penny knelt down to look at him closely.

"Tammylan! He has got the loveliest eyes!" she cried. "They are like jewels — and they look so wise and kind."

"Yes — he's a wise old fellow is Bufo," said Tammylan. "Come along, old chap — up on my knee."

The toad levered himself up and stood on his hind-legs, resting his forepaws on Tammylan's leg. Then he crawled slowly up to the knee. Tammylan took a piece of heather stem and gently tickled the toad on his back. Bufo at once put an arm behind himself and scratched where Tammylan had tickled. The children laughed.

"Now see the difference between this frog and my toad," said the wild man. "See the frog's smooth, shiny, rather moist body, and its greeny-brown colouring—and now see the toad's earthy colour, and his dry, pimply skin. He is quite different. Look at his back legs, too—they are much shorter than the frog's. The frog's long hind-legs give him the power of jumping very high in the air, to frighten his enemies and to escape easily—but the toad can only hop with difficulty and usually crawls."

"Well, how does he get away from his enemies, then?" asked Benjy. Tammylan was just about to answer when the toad replied for him—for Scamper, the squirrel, suddenly dropped down on the toad in play—and then, in a trice, the squirrel gave a distressed cry, rubbed its little

mouth, and leapt to a ledge above the children, its mouth open, and foam and bubbles dripping out at the sides.

"Oh! Whatever's the matter with Scamper?" cried Benjy in dismay. Tammylan laughed.

"Don't worry about him!" he said. "Old Bufo, the toad, has just taught him that toads cannot be played with in that manner! As soon as Scamper dropped down on him the toad sent out an evil-tasting fluid from some of those pimples on his back — so horrible that no enemy will take a second lick, and certainly not a bite!" Scamper will soon be all right."

The toad lay crouched on Tammylan's knee, keeping quite still, as if it were dead. "It's an old trick of the toad's, to pretend that it is just a clod of earth," said Tammylan. "Now — do you see that bluebottle fly? Watch what happens when it perches near the frog or the toad."

The bluebottle fly buzzed around. The frog heard it and became alert. The toad heard it, too, but made no sign. The fly flew down on Tammylan's knee.

And then, it just wasn't there!

"What's happened to it?" cried Sheila. "I didn't see it fly away!"

"*I* saw what happened," said Benjy. "The frog flipped out its tongue, struck the fly with it — and flipped it into its mouth. It blinked its eyes and swallowed. Isn't that right, Tammylan?"

"Yes," said Tammylan. "You have quick eyes, Benjy! The frog's tongue is fastened to the *front* of his mouth, not to the back as ours is — so, when a fly comes, the frog opens his mouth, flips out his tongue to its full length, and strikes the fly with the sticky tip. That's the end of the fly. It all happens so quickly that it really seems as if the fly has disappeared by magic!"

"There's another fly!" said Benjy. "It's going near the toad — oh — it's gone!"

That time it was Bufo, the toad, who had flicked out a tongue and caught the fly. It was all done in the twinkling of an eye, so fast that it was difficult to follow.

Benjy tickled Bufo's back. The toad liked it. Penny tickled the frog — but, with a bound, it was off Tammylan's knee, and leapt towards a patch of wet grass as fast as it could go.

Tammylan put the toad down on the ground. "You can go home, Bufo," he said. The toad crawled to its hiding-place under the stone and disappeared.

"He lived there all last summer, slept there all the winter, and now lives there this summer," said Tammylan. "I am fond of him — a quiet, wise old thing, who never hurries, never worries, and just gives a croak now and again to remind me that he is near me!"

A croak came from under the stone. The children laughed. "He heard what you said," said Penny.

"When you next go by the pond, look for the other member of the frog family — the newt," said Tammylan. "He has a long tail, but please don't mix him up with the lizards you saw the other day! Maybe you will be lucky enough to see the great crested newt, which looks like a miniature dragon, with its toothed crest running all down its back, and its brilliant under-colouring."

"We'll look," promised Benjy. "I think we ought to get back now, Tammylan. It's stopped raining, and the storm has quite gone. There is blue sky over there."

The wind had almost dried Penny's frock, but Tammylan said she had better keep his old rug wrapped round her. The others had had coats, which they had taken off to dry, but Penny had come out without one. So, clad in

Tammylan's old red rug Penny went home with the others, feeling rather like a Red Indian as she capered along.

The lane was almost clear of frogs and toads when the children once more ran down it.

"They've each found a little place for themselves," said Benjy. "Somewhere they are hiding, and watching for flies. How I wish I had a tongue I could flip out like a frog's."

They practised tongue-flipping all the way home, much to the surprise of everyone they met. Auntie Bess soon stopped them!

"It may not be rude in frogs!" she said, "but it's certainly not good manners in children. Stop it, all of you!"

XIX

FLITTERMOUSE THE BAT

The summer days slid by, golden and warm. It seemed to the children as if they had always lived at Cherry-Tree Farm. London seemed to them a misty place, not quite real.

Their mother and father were having a grand time in America, and were supposed to come back at the end of the summer. Then the children would have to return to London.

When September came in, with its ripening fruit, its peaceful blue skies and heavy morning dews, the children were very happy. They were allowed to pick what ripe fruit they liked, so they had a glorious time.

But gradually Benjy became quiet and sad looking. The others couldn't understand it. Was Benjy ill?

"He just won't laugh or make jokes any more," said Rory. "I think he *must* be ill."

But Benjy wasn't ill—he was just thinking that soon, very soon, the four of them would have to say good-bye to the farm and go back to town. He was counting the precious days. He wondered if Scamper would be allowed in London. He looked at the solemn cows he knew so well, the quacking ducks, the old brown horses with their shaggy heels, and inside him was a horrible ache.

Aunt Bess was really worried about Benjy—and she thought that he must be homesick for his home in London and his father and mother! So she kept talking in a very bright voice about London, and that it wouldn't be long before he was back there, and things like that; all of which made Benjy feel a hundred times worse, of course!

And then one day Auntie Bess got a letter from America at breakfast-time, and read it with a very surprised look.

"Is it from Mother and Daddy?" asked Rory.

"Yes," said Aunt Bess. "I am afraid you will all be very disappointed with the news — they aren't coming back until Christmas!"

"Oh!" said Penny, looking ready to cry. "Oh, I did think they would come back soon."

Rory frowned. "I think they might come back this month, as they said they would," he said.

"We've been without them such a long time," said Sheila.

Benjy said nothing at all. Auntie Bess wondered what he was thinking.

"Poor Benjy," she said. "I'm afraid it will all be a great disappointment to you. You can't go back to London now, and I know you wanted to."

Benjy stared at his aunt as if he couldn't believe his ears. "Can't go back to *London*!" he said. "Are we going to stay on at Cherry-Tree Farm, then?"

"I'm afraid so," said Aunt Bess. "I shall love to have you, but I know that you . . ."

What she was going to say nobody ever knew, for Benjy suddenly went quite completely mad. He jumped up from the table, knocking over the salt and the pepper, and capered round the room like a Red Indian doing a war-dance. He shouted and sang, and everyone stared at him in amazement.

"So you *didn't* want to go back!" said Aunt Bess, in surprise. "And all this time I've been thinking you've been so quiet and glum because you wanted to go home!"

"Oh, Aunt Bess, no, no, no!" shouted Benjy. "You're

138

quite wrong. "I never, never want to leave Cherry-Tree Farm for London. Oh, oh, to think we'll be here till Christmas now! How gorgeous! How marvellous! How . . ."

Everyone began to laugh, for Benjy looked so funny leaping round the breakfast table. Scamper, the squirrel, was quite scared and rushed to the top of the curtain, where he sat barking and stamping.

"Well, now we've settled that, come back and finish your breakfast, Benjy," said Uncle Tim, who was just as amused, and as pleased, as Aunt Bess. "What about their schooling, Bess? They can't miss another term."

"I'm to make arrangements for them to go to the vicar's for lessons," said Aunt Bess, looking at the letter. "You know, he already has five other pupils, and our four can join them. They will like the walk across the fields each day—won't you, children?"

"Oh *yes!*" cried everyone, hardly able to believe so much good news all at once. Lessons at the lovely old vicarage—Cherry-Tree Farm all the autumn—it was too good to be true. The only pity was that they wouldn't see their parents for so long. Still, they could look forward to Christmas!

"We must go and tell old Tammylan the good news as soon as we can," said Benjy after breakfast. "We'll go to-night. He said he would be away over the hill all to-day."

So that evening, when the sun sent slanting yellow rays over the fields, and the trees had long shadows behind them, the four children and Scamper set out to Tammylan's tree-house. They took their supper with them—big bottles of creamy milk, and hunks of new bread with home-made cream cheese to eat with it. They took some for Tammylan too, for he loved milk and cheese.

Tammylan was sitting outside his house, watching the

fish jumping in the river. He smiled at the children, and saw at once that they had news.

"Tammylan — we're staying till Christmas! What do you think of that?" said Benjy, grinning. "We're to have lessons with the vicar — not to be sent away to school! Are you glad?"

"Very," said Tammylan. "There will be time for you to have a few more lessons with *me* too!"

"Lessons with you?" said Penny in surprise. "What sort of lessons?"

"The same as I've given you before," said Tammylan. "Teaching you to make friends with the little folk of the countryside! There are still a few more people you don't know yet, Penny."

"But there *can't* be!" said Penny. "Why, we know the squirrels, and the snakes, the badgers and the otter, the water-vole and the slow-worm, the . . ."

"Well, here's one you don't know yet!" said Tammylan, as a little bat swooped down near Sheila. It almost touched her and she screamed.

"Oh! Oh! A bat! Make it go away, quick!"

The bat came back again and fluttered round Sheila's head on its curious wings. Sheila screamed again, and hit out at it with her hand. "Tammylan! Don't sit there like that! Make it go away! It will get into my hair!"

Tammylan looked cross. He didn't move at all. "The only time I ever feel I want to give you a good slap, Sheila, is when you screech like that about nothing," he said. "Be quiet!"

Sheila got such a shock. She stopped squealing and looked ashamed. She went very red and tried not to look at Tammylan. "Sorry," she said.

"I should think so!" said Tammylan. "Now, will you

please tell me exactly why you behaved like that, squealing and screaming at a tiny creature that can neither sting nor bite?"

"Well, Tammylan," began Sheila. "I'm afraid of bats."

"Why?" asked Tammylan.

"Because . . ." said Sheila and then she stopped and thought. She really didn't know why she was afraid of them! "Well, you see . . ." she went on, "I've seen people cower away from bats, and I've heard people say they get into your hair."

"Well, they don't get into your hair, and they are perfectly harmless," said Tammylan. "Please don't act like that again, Sheila. It's no wonder animals and birds won't make friends with you. All animals sense when anyone fears them — and see what your squealing has done to Scamper. He's really scared!"

The squirrel was sitting on the top of the house, trembling. Benjy got up and lifted him off. The little creature cuddled under his arm-pit, digging his paws into Benjy's shirt.

"We'll show Sheila what an extraordinary little thing a bat really is," said Tammylan, getting up. "If she sees one closely maybe she won't be quite so frightened. They are marvellously made!"

"Can you make them come to you, Tammylan?" asked Benjy, surprised.

"I can make them fly near me, but I cannot make them come to my hand whilst you are here," said the wild man. "I am going to get my net — I can easily catch one with that."

He went into the tree-house and came out with a kind of butterfly net. He stood by the doorway, and made some extremely high-sounding squeaks in his throat. Benjy

141

pricked up his ears. "I've heard the bats squeaking like that," he said.

"Then you have sharp ears, Benjy," said Tammylan. None of the others could hear the bats answering Tammylan. Only Benjy's sharp ears heard them. They came fluttering down around Tammylan's head. With a quick dart of his net he caught one. He sat down, and took the little quivering creature from the net.

Whenever any animal felt Tammylan's gentle, strong hands about it all fear left it and it was peaceful and safe. The bat lay in Tammylan's brown hand, and the children crowded round to look at it.

"It's not a kind of bird, after all," said Penny. "I thought it was!"

"Oh no," said Tammylan. "There is nothing of the bird about it, except its aerial life. It has no feathers."

"It's like a tiny mouse with big black wings," said Benjy.

"Country folk call it the flittermouse," said Tammylan, "and it's really not a bad name for it. Look at its tiny furry body."

"And look at its big wings!" cried Sheila. "What are they made of, if they are not feathery wings, Tammylan?"

Tammylan gently spread out the bat's strange wing. "Look," he said, "do you see how long the bat's fingers have grown? It is those that support the wing, which is simply a broad web of skin, stretched over the finger-bones and joined to the bat's little body. The bat flies with its fingers, over which the skin has grown!"

"How strange!" said Rory, who, like the others, had never seen a bat closely before. "What's this little hook thing at the tip of the wings, Tammylan?"

"That is the bat's thumb, one on each wing," said

Tammylan. "That little hook, with which the bat can hang on to any surface, is all that is left of its thumb — but it finds it very useful."

"Well, I never knew what a queer thing could be done with fingers and thumb before!" said Sheila, who was not a bit afraid of the bat now that she could see it closely for what it was. "Look — there's a little pouch between the legs and tail, Tammylan. What's that for?"

"That's where the bat puts his beetles and flies, when he catches them!" said Tammylan. "It's his pocket! Watch the bats that are flying overhead, Sheila — when they suddenly swoop and dip down, you will know they are catching an insect and pouching it!"

The four children watched. "I think they fly almost better than birds do," said Benjy. "That bat up there stopped in mid-air just now — just completely stopped! I've never seen a bird do that."

"They certainly fly marvellously well," said Tammylan. "They are a joy to watch. Do you see how closely they fly to the trees and yet never touch them? They have a wonderful sense of the nearness of things."

Tammylan set free the tiny bat he had caught. It flew off to join the others. "That was a little common bat," said Tammylan. "There are plenty of other kinds, but unless we catch them and examine them it is difficult to point them out in this twilight."

"I never see bats in the winter," said Benjy. "They sleep then, don't they?"

"Yes," said Tammylan. "They get nice and fat in the autumn, and then hide themselves away in some cave or hollow tree or old barn. Do you know that old tumbledown barn at the end of the long field, at Cherry-Tree Farm? Well, hundreds of bats sleep there, not only during the winter, but during the daytime now, as well."

"I shall look in and see!" said Benjy, pleased.

"Well, you won't stay long!" said Tammylan. But he wouldn't tell Benjy why.

They had their supper outside the tree-house in the September twilight. Tammylan enjoyed the bread and cheese and the creamy milk. He gave the children a basketful of sweet wild strawberries to eat. They were delicious.

"I picked them to-day for you," said Tammylan. "I hoped you would come to-night."

When the first stars came out Tammylan said they must go, so they said good-bye and walked slowly home in the deepening twilight.

"I shall just look in that old barn as we go by," said Benjy. So when they came to it they all went inside — but, just as Tammylan had said, they didn't stay long!

"Pooh! The *smell!*" said Benjy, holding his nose. "Well, if that's what bats' sleeping-places smell like I shan't ever want to spend a winter with *them*."

The bats squeaked round his head as if they were laughing at Benjy — and this time even Sheila did not mind them. She had learnt her lesson, and would never be so silly as to squeal and screech again!

XX

PENNY'S PRICKLY PET

There was one thing that Penny longed and longed for — and that was a pet of her own. She loved Scamper, the squirrel, who was growing fast now and was a real pet of the family, though it was always Benjy he cuddled up to. She loved Shadow, the collie, and the big white cat by the fire. She liked the stable-cats too, but they were half-wild and wouldn't stay to be stroked.

"But none of them really belong to *me*," thought Penny. "I want something of my own — and I'd like a wild animal, like Benjy has."

She wondered if she could find a young badger, or a fox-cub. But Uncle Tim put his foot down at once.

"A fox-cub!" he said in disgust. "What next? It's all very well whilst they're cubs — nice little playful things they are then — but they grow up, Penny, they grow up! And what are you going to do with a full-grown tame fox, I'd like to know? Keep it on collar and chain, like a dog?"

"Oh *no*!" said Penny, shocked. "I'd tame it properly and let it run loose, Uncle Tim."

"And do you know what it would do?" said her uncle. "It would catch all your aunt's hens and ducks! It would go to the farms around and eat the hens and ducks there too. It would be the greatest nuisance in the world, and it would have to be shot."

"Oh, I won't have a tame fox then," said Penny. "I didn't think about it eating hens and things. I promise you I won't have a fox-cub, Uncle."

And then Penny found a pet, quite unexpectedly. What

do you suppose it was! A hedgehog!

Penny got up early one morning and went round by the tennis-court to pick a ripe plum. As she ran round the tennis-netting she noticed what looked like a big brown lump of earth rolled up in the edge. She went to it—and to her great surprise she found that a hedgehog had got caught in the netting and was so tangled up that it couldn't get out! It had curled itself up tightly and lay as if it were dead; perfectly still.

"Oh, the poor thing! Oh, quick, come and help it!" shouted Penny. "Benjy, Benjy, where are you?"

But nobody came. So Penny fetched a pair of garden scissors from the tool-house and hacked away at the net until she had freed the hedgehog.

Still it didn't move.

Penny tried to lift it up. It was very prickly indeed. It was just like a round ball of spines, and the little girl had to put the funny animal into her overall before she could carry it.

Then she noticed that fleas were jumping from it and she dropped it in horror.

Benjy came running up just then and was surprised to see the hedgehog. "You needn't worry about the fleas," he said. "They aren't the kind to bite *us*. But, wait a minute —I'll just dust the hedgehog with the insect powder that Aunt Bess uses for Shadow. That will soon clean up the hedgehog!"

He got the tin and dusted the powder over the hedgehog. The fleas all leapt off in horror and died. The hedgehog couldn't bear the smell of the powder and he uncurled himself very suddenly.

"Oh!" cried Penny, "look at him! He's undone himself! Hasn't he got a dear little face—and such bright eyes. I like him. Look, he's running along — doesn't he go fast? Benjy, he shall be my pet!"

"Goodness! What a funny pet!" said Benjy with a grin. "You'll need to wear armour whenever you want to cuddle him, Penny. I'll go and get him some bread and milk. I've heard the hedgehogs love that. See that he doesn't get too far."

But before Benjy came back Penny had had to put the hedgehog into a hen-coop, for he got along so fast she was afraid she might lose him! There he was, sitting in the hen-coop, looking at Penny with bright eyes.

He loved the bread and milk, and almost tipped it over to get at it. The children watched him in delight.

"I shall take him to Tammylan this morning," said Penny. "He will like to see my new pet. Let's go and tell Auntie Bess."

Aunt Bess laughed when she heard about the hedgehog. "They are useful creatures in a garden," she said. "They eat all kinds of insects, and slugs and snails. I once had a plague of cockroach beetles down in the cellar — and your uncle got me a hedgehog and put him down there. Well, in a week there wasn't a cockroach to be seen!"

"I think he'll make a nice pet, don't you?" said Penny. "I'll give him bread and milk every day."

But a great disappointment was in store for poor Penny — for when she went to take her hedgehog from the hen-coop to show him to Tammylan, he was gone!

The hen-coop was quite empty. The little girl stared through the bars of the coop in dismay. "Has anyone let out my hedgehog?" she cried. But nobody had. It was most mysterious. And then Uncle Tim explained it all.

"He could easily get out between the bars, Penny," said her uncle. "All he would have to do would be to put down his spines and squeeze through! You've lost him, I'm afraid. Never mind!"

But Penny did mind. She didn't say anything, but she went into the dark cowshed and cried by herself. Then she decided to go and see Tammylan and tell him about it. So she slipped off by herself to the tree-house — but she met Tammylan long before she got there. He was sitting by the stream, watching some water-hens.

"Hallo, Penny," he said. "You've been crying! What's the matter?"

"It's my hedgehog," said Penny, sitting down beside

the wild man. "I meant to keep him for a pet—and now he's gone."

Tammylan listened to the whole story. He didn't seem at all surprised to hear that the little girl's hedgehog had gone.

"You know, Penny, it's rather difficult to make a pet of a grown hedgehog," he said. "You should begin with a baby—then you can teach him to know you and not to escape."

"But how can I find a baby one?" asked Penny.

"Oh, I can easily get you one," said the wild man. "Come along—we'll see if we can find you a tiny one to take home!"

Penny skipped along beside Tammylan in the greatest delight. You never knew what he was going to say or do—he was the most exciting man in the world!

Tammylan led Penny over a field, and came at last to a steep bank, which was overhung by bushes and briars. Tammylan pressed back some brambles and Penny saw the opening of a small hole, partly hidden by some green moss.

Tammylan put aside the moss and made a small grunting noise. At once a blunt nose looked out, and Penny saw the bright eyes of a hedgehog looking up at her and Tammylan.

"This is a mother hedgehog," explained Tammylan. "She has five youngsters in this hole with her. They are about a month old, perhaps a little more. She made a cosy home for them in this old wasps' nest-hole. She took moss and leaves into the hole with her mouth, and her small family live there happily. She will soon take them out at night to teach them how to hunt for beetles and slugs—and perhaps to nibble a few of the toadstools that are coming up everywhere now."

Tammylan put his hand into the hole, and felt about. He brought it out again and in it Penny saw a very small hedgehog indeed!

"Oh, its prickles are quite soft and pale!" cried Penny.

"Yes," said Tammylan. "They will gradually darken and become stiff, but the hedgehog will have to wait many months before it can erect its spines properly and protect itself with them. Now, Penny — would you like this tiny hedgehog for a pet? It will soon know you and will stay in the garden or somewhere nearby when it grows up."

"Oh, I'd love it," said Penny. "The others will laugh at me, I know, for having such a prickly baby, but it will be *mine*! What shall I feed it on?"

"Milk," said Tammylan, putting the tiny creature into Penny's hands. "Ask Rory to lend you his fountain-pen filler. Fill it with milk and squirt it gently into the hedgehog's mouth. When it has grown a little it will feed itself from a bread-and-milk bowl. And after that it will hunt around the garden for beetles and slugs."

"Does it sleep in the winter?" asked Penny, carrying the hedgehog very carefully.

"Oh yes," said Tammylan. "It likes a hole rather like the one we took it from — but if you make it a sleeping place in a box, lined with dead leaves and moss, it will sleep there till the spring. What will you call it?"

"Prickles," said Penny at once. "I'll take it home now, Tammylan, and give it some milk. Thank you so much for giving it to me. I shall take great care of it and make it just as happy as Scamper, the squirrel, is."

She went off with the hedgehog — and the others were half-jealous when they looked at it and heard Penny's story. Rory got his fountain-pen filler at once and Penny filled it with milk. She gently squirted some into the tiny creature's mouth. It spluttered and choked a little, but liked the milk very much. Then Benjy went off to make it a kind of cage to run about in, and Rory and Sheila hunted for little stones and moss.

Its home was soon ready—and the children were pleased to see the tiny animal curl up on the moss and go to sleep quite happily.

"It doesn't seem to miss its mother," said Sheila. "Well, Penny—you've got what you wanted—a pet of your own, though I do think it's a funny one. I hope you'll never ask me to cuddle it for you!"

XXI

THE BATTLE OF THE STAGS

In late September the children began to have lessons again.

They walked across the field to the vicarage, and loved the peaceful autumn countryside. They liked their lessons in the quiet study of the old vicar, who, with four or five other pupils, enjoyed teaching the four children from the farm.

They could not go and see Tammylan quite so often now, for they had homework to do. They saw him one afternoon, on their way to the farm for tea, and called to him.

"Tammylan! Wait for us! We want to ask you something!"

Tammylan waited. They ran up to him.

"Tammylan! We found such a lot of funny little dead creatures in the fields this week!" cried Benjy. "They had long noses. What are they?"

"Do you mean little creatures like that one on the bank?" asked Tammylan. The children looked — and there, on the bank, lay a little dead animal, looking rather like a mouse with a long nose.

"Yes," said Benjy. "What is it?"

"It's one of the smallest of our animals," said Tammylan, picking it up. "It's a little shrew. You can always tell a shrew by its long, movable nose. Now, just keep quiet for a minute. I think I saw one moving here."

They kept quiet — and sure enough a tiny shrew came out from its hiding-place, moving its long flexible nose.

152

It was a dear little thing, and did not seem to see the children and Tammylan at all.

"They are short-sighted," said Tammylan in a low voice. "See this one looking for a caterpillar or beetle. He is always hungry!"

"Why are there so many dead this autumn?" asked Benjy. "I don't like to see them."

"They only live for fourteen or fifteen months," said Tammylan. "They have a busy, happy little life, and then, before the bitter winter comes to visit them for the second time, they lay themselves down and die."

"Tammylan, I saw a dormouse yesterday evening," said Penny. "It was in one of Uncle's frames!"

"Oh, that reminds me—you must meet a new friend of mine!" said Tammylan. He wriggled himself a little, and a bright-eyed mouse came down from one of his sleeves. It was a fat little dormouse!

The children were thrilled. Really, you never knew what Tammylan was going to produce next! Benjy tickled the pretty dormouse down its back.

"Isn't it fat?" he said.

"Yes—like most of the winter sleepers the dormouse likes to get itself fat and healthy before its nap," said Tammylan. "I expect the one you saw in your uncle's frame was looking about for a warm place for the winter, Penny."

Tammylan took a hazel nut from his pocket and cracked it. It was not yet quite ripe, but the little dormouse took the white kernel and ate it in delight. Then it ran back up Tammylan's sleeve and disappeared.

"Where is it?" asked Penny, and she prodded the wild man's arm till she found where the dormouse had curled itself up. "I do wish I had a dormouse living up my sleeve too," she said. "Tammylan, my little hedgehog is growing. He is getting more prickly, and he drinks such a lot of milk now!"

"Good," said Tammylan. "Well, perhaps I shall see you all soon again. Don't come on Saturday because I am going over the hills to see the red deer."

"The red deer!" exclaimed Benjy. "I'd like to see them too. I knew there were some about because Uncle told me once he had a whole field of turnips spoilt by them. They came in the night and ate them."

"Very likely," said Tammylan. "Well, if you want to come with me be at the stile at nine o'clock sharp. It's a good long walk, so you'll have to bring your lunch."

All the children wanted to go. They had never seen deer except in the Zoo. They made up their minds to ask Aunt Bess for a picnic lunch and to meet Tammylan at the stile without fail on Saturday.

It was a marvellous October day when the children stood at the stile waiting for Tammylan. It had rained every day since they had seen him, but now it had cleared up and the sun shone almost as hotly as summer. A few trees had turned colour and they shone brilliantly in the autumn sunshine.

"The sunshine always looks much yellower in the autumn than in the summer," said Sheila. "I say, look at those enormous blackberries! Let's pick some whilst we're waiting."

They were so busy eating the juicy berries that they didn't notice Tammylan till he was just behind them. "So you've come!" said Tammylan. "Good! We ought to see a bit of fun to-day! The red stags have their wonderful antlers now, and maybe we shall see them using them as weapons! It is the time of year when the red deer fight for leadership."

"I say! How thrilling!" said Rory. "Come on, let's hurry!"

Tammylan led the way over the hill and across a wide stretch of common. Then there came another set of heather-covered hills. Penny was quite out of breath at the top, for her legs were not so long as the others were. They sat down at the top for a rest. The countryside spread out below them, green and gold, changing to a purple blue in the distance.

"Do you see that dip in the moors over there?" said Tammylan, pointing to a wild-looking stretch of moorland. "Well, I think we shall find our deer there to-day."

No sooner had he finished speaking than a strange noise came on the wind. It was like a loud bellow, a ringing sound that echoed all around.

"What's that?" asked Penny, looking startled.

"That's a stag sending out his challenge to all others," said Tammylan. "Come along. I know there are two or three stags about here, as well as a good many hinds — those are the mother deer, you know. We shall be in time to see the stags battling with one another if we hurry."

Another bellowing cry came over the moors as the children followed Tammylan, and then another and another.

"Look!" said Benjy, "there's a stag!"

They all looked — and there, on the brow of a small hill, stood a magnificent red deer, his great antlers standing up proudly on his head.

"Oh!" said Rory, "what a splendid animal he is!"

"Will he hurt us?" asked Penny, rather anxiously.

"Well, we certainly won't go too near him!" said Tammylan. "Ah, look — here comes another stag to challenge him!"

A second deer came slowly up the hill. He threw back his antlers and sent out his cry. The first stag pawed the ground in excitement—then he ran straight at his enemy! The two put down their heads and there was a loud clash as their enormous antlers crashed together.

"Their antlers have caught in one another!" said Rory, excited.

So they had. The two stags pushed and pulled, stamped and strained at each other—and the antlers at last freed themselves. But not for long—once again the stags rushed at one another, and the antlers rattled.

"I wonder they don't break!" said Sheila. "Why are they fighting, Tammylan?"

"They are fighting to see who is the strongest and who will be leader of the herd," said Tammylan. "Only the strongest guards the hinds. Both these stags are young and strong, and each wants to be the leader."

"Look! Are those the hinds over there?" cried Benjy, pointing to a hill not far off, where a group of deer stood watching the fierce battle. They had no antlers, and were rather smaller than the stags.

"Yes," said Tammylan. "Ah, look—one stag is winning. He is pressing the other down the hill. He is the stronger of the two!"

For a while the two stags struggled and panted, but gradually the weaker one gave way, and when he saw a chance, he fled. The victorious stag sent a ringing cry after him, then stamped over to the herd. He was king for that season!

"I wish I could see the stag's lovely antlers a bit closer," said Benjy. "They look like a tree on his head. Does it take years and years to grow them as long as that, Tammylan?"

"No," said Tammylan, "it usually takes a stag ten weeks."

"Ten weeks!" cried Benjy, in surprise. "No, Tammylan, you're joking—those enormous antlers would take ten years to grow!"

"A stag's antlers are a marvellous growth," said Tammylan. "He throws them off each year, and grows them again—and each year they are a little bigger, to show that he is older!"

"Did that stag who won the battle grow new antlers this spring then?" asked Rory.

"Yes," said Tammylan. "On his head, if you could have seen him this spring, you would have been able to feel two very hot knobs. From these knobs the antlers began to grow—as fast as the bracken grows in the wood! Then the growing antlers branch out—more branches come—and by the time that the ten weeks are gone he has on his head the great antlers you see now! At first these growing antlers are covered by a mossy kind of skin, called the *velvet*—but when the antlers are full grown the stag rubs off the velvet against the trunk of trees. I have often seen it hanging there in the summer."

"Well, cows don't throw away their horns every spring!" said Rory. "I wish they did. I'd make a nice collection of them!"

"I should think the stags must find their antlers a great nuisance when they run through the woods," said Sheila. "They must catch in the tree-branches."

"Well, they don't," said Tammylan. "The stags throw their heads back so that their antlers lie on their back—they don't catch in the trees at all—in fact, the antlers save them from many a bruise!"

"Where do stags put their horns when they throw them

158

off?" asked Sheila.

"Would you like to see if we can find some?" asked Tammylan. "Well, come along. The stags always feel ill and weak when they are shedding their antlers, and often they go to some cave and lie there. I know an old cave near here where I found a pair of antlers one year. We'll go and see if there are any this time."

So off they went to a nearby hill where there was a narrow cave. It opened out into a wide chamber at the end, and smelt of bats. Rory had a torch and flashed it round. He gave a shout.

"Here's one! Look! A fine antler!"

He took it out into the sunshine to see. It was a magnificent antler, quite perfect. "It is the antler of a full-grown stag," said Tammylan, looking at it. "Count the points — I should think there are about forty."

"Can I keep it for myself?" asked Rory, in excitement. "My word — what will the boys in London say to this!"

"I wish I could have one too!" said Sheila, and she took Rory's torch. She ran back into the cave, trying not to smell the sour bat-smell there. She flashed the torch round — and to her great delight saw a fallen antler in one corner. She picked it up and raced outside with it.

"Here's the pair to your antler!" she cried. "Look!"

"Oh, give it to me — now I shall have two!" cried Rory, and he snatched the other antler from Sheila. She gave an angry cry.

"No, Rory! It's mine. I found it and I want it!"

"But it's a pair. I must have a pair!" cried Rory. "Mustn't I, Tammylan?"

"It would certainly be nice to have a matching pair of antlers," said Tammylan, in a dry sort of voice. "But that isn't a pair. It is two odd ones."

"How do you know?" said Rory—but almost at once he saw what Tammylan meant. The antler that Sheila had found was not so big nor so branched. It certainly could not have been worn by the same deer that wore Rory's antler.

"This antler was worn by a four-year-old stag," said Tammylan. "It doesn't show the fifth-year branch. Well, you can keep it, Sheila. It's an odd one, like Rory's."

Sheila was thrilled. She tucked the antler under her arm and danced round.

"Benjy's got a squirrel, Penny's got a hedgehog, and Rory and I have antlers! Now we've all got something."

Scamper, the squirrel, chattered a little and tried to get inside a bag of food that Benjy was carrying. Benjy laughed.

"Scamper says it's time for a meal!" he said. "Where shall we have it?"

"I know a sunny place, where there are many birds and voles to watch," said Tammylan. "Let's go there. It will be fun to eat and watch things at the same time."

"Come on, then," said Rory. "I'm hungry enough to eat all we've got!"

XXII

A QUEER PERFORMANCE

It wasn't long before they were all sitting down on a
grassy bank, sheltered by great clumps of gorse and
bramble. Penny's mouth watered when she saw the
clusters of ripe blackberries on the brambles and she
made up her mind to do a little picking afterwards!

It was a gorgeous lunch. Aunt Bess had made ham
sandwiches with a dab of mustard on each, and there
were late tomatoes to bite into, nice and juicy. There
were slices of plum cake, spicy and rich, and some eating
plums as sweet as sugar. Scamper sucked a tomato, and
made such a noise.

"I shall really have to teach you manners, Scamper!"
said Benjy.

There were plenty of birds about, just as Tammylan
had said. A robin flew down at their feet. Some chaffinches
flew over the hedge, crying "pink-pink!" A blackbird
cocked a bright eye at them, and some thrushes sang a
little from nearby trees.

There were voles too, running here and there, and even
a daring rabbit, who came out of his burrow to watch the
children. A tiny mouse ran under the hedge and another
peeped at them from a tuft of grass. It was fun to eat and
look round at so many little creatures.

"I wonder what's in that pile of brushwood over there,"
Rory said, as he ate his plum cake. "I am sure there's
something. I thought I saw some eyes looking at me just
now."

"I'll go and see," said Sheila, who had finished her

lunch. She got up and went slowly to the heap of old wood. As she got there, a snake-like head looked out at her, and she heard a loud hissing noise. She ran back to the others at once.

"I think it's a snake," she said. "It hissed at me."

"I don't think it is," said Tammylan. "We'll wait for a minute and see."

So they all sat quiet and waited. Presently a tiny vole ran across the grass near to the brushwood. A long slender body immediately threw itself from its hiding-place, and pounced on the vole. But, with a squeak, the vole turned sideways and darted into a small hole.

"It's a weasel!" said Tammylan. "The farmer's friend. He will rid a farm of rats and mice if he is given a chance, though he will not say no to a chicken if the hen-house has a place for him to squeeze inside!"

The weasel looked at the group of children and hissed again. He really was rather snake-like, for he had a small head, long neck, short legs and slender body, and he moved with an easy gliding motion.

"I've no doubt Master Weasel is hungry to-day, for some reason or other," said Tammylan. "He doesn't look in very good condition—perhaps he is getting old and finds it more difficult to hunt. Weasels, as a rule, are marvellous hunters, quite fearless and very fierce."

The children looked at the hissing animal. It wasn't very big, only about ten inches long, with a short tail. It wore a red-brown coat, and was white underneath.

"I say, look! There's another weasel!" said Rory, nodding towards a hedge. Sure enough, a second animal was there, looking as fierce as the weasel. Tammylan took a look at it.

"No—that's a stoat," he said. "They *are* a little alike—

but the stoat is distinctly larger. Look at his tail too — it's longer and has a black tip."

"Well, I can see the difference now, when *both* the creatures are there to look at," said Rory. "But I'm sure if I met one alone I wouldn't know which it was!"

"I'll tell you an old rhyme about the stoat and the weasel," said Tammylan. "I don't know who made it up, but it's very good. Listen.

> *'The stoat can be easily*
> *Told from the weasel*
> *By the simple fact*
> *That his tail is blacked*
> *And his figure*
> *Is slightly the bigger!'"*

The children laughed. "That's very good!" said Sheila, and she repeated the rhyme correctly, for she had a very good memory. "Now I shall never forget which is the stoat and which is the weasel — whenever I see one I shall just say the rhyme to myself and I'll know!"

The stoat had seen the weasel and was angry. It snarled and ran into the open, taking no notice of the group of children. It, too, looked rather snake-like as it went, for it did not exactly run, but went along with low bounds.

"Will they fight?" asked Rory, thinking that it would be a real day for fights, if so.

"No," said Tammylan. "The stoat won't waste its time on a weasel. It knows that the weasel would simply fight till both creatures were dead! It is angry to see it here because it probably thinks that this is its own private hunting-ground. It doesn't want to share it with a fierce little weasel!"

"I suppose it hunts all the year round," said Benjy. "I can't imagine either the weasel or the stoat going to sleep for long!"

"You're right!" said Tammylan. "They are fiercer in the winter than in the summer. In the cold north country the stoat does a queer thing in the winter—he changes to white, and becomes the ermine!"

"How funny!" said Penny, staring. "Why does he do that?"

"Well, I really think you might find out the reason for yourself!" said Tammylan.

Penny thought. "Yes—I know why," she said. "It's because snow lies on the ground in the north for a long time, and the stoat would be easily seen in his *brown* coat—so he puts on a white one to hide himself!"

"Good girl!" said Tammylan, pleased. "Yes—his coat changes like magic. But down here, where it is warmer and we do not often have a winter where the snow lies for long, the stoat does not bother to change his coat. I have sometimes seen him when he has changed to an ermine up in the north, and is all in white—all I could see against the snow was a pair of eyes and the black tip of his tail!"

The stoat suddenly sniffed the air. He evidently smelt something good, for in a trice he was bounding off, and disappeared through a hole in the hedge.

"He smelt his dinner somewhere!" said Benjy with a laugh. "The weasel is glad to see him go."

"I think the weasel is just about to perform for us," said Tammylan. "Keep quite quiet now and you will see something strange."

The weasel was certainly behaving very queerly. He had come out farther into the open, and was doing most extraordinary things. He ran round and round as if he were chasing his own short tail. He jumped up in the air and down. He wriggled his body like a snake, and threw himself over and over. The children watched, quite fascinated.

"What is he doing?" asked Penny, in a whisper.

"He wants to amaze all the birds and animals round about," whispered back Tammylan. "He wants them to come nearer and nearer to look at him. Then he will pounce—and get his dinner!"

The weasel went on and on. The birds in the hedgerow stopped their singing to watch. They couldn't take their eyes off the extraordinary weasel. They had never seen such a thing before.

The weasel wriggled and ran round himself. A small vole popped his head out of a hole and watched. A mouse looked on in amazement and went a little nearer to see what was happening. A big blackbird flew down to inspect the performance.

Then two sparrows fluttered down and a chaffinch. They all watched, quite still. The children could not stop watching either—and although they longed to warn the birds and little animals they could not open their mouths to say a word! It seemed as if the weasel was putting a

165

spell on everything and everyone. It was very strange.

The weasel went on and on with his performance — and he got gradually nearer to the fat blackbird. The bird did not move, but looked at the wriggling animal. Penny wanted to call out but she couldn't. Everyone seemed to have their eyes glued on the extraordinary weasel.

And now the weasel was almost within striking distance of the foolish blackbird — and then Tammylan broke the spell. He clapped his hands — and at once the blackbird flew off, sending out his ringing alarm-call! All the other birds flew high into the trees, and every mouse and vole disappeared as if by magic. Even the weasel jumped with fright.

As for the children they jumped even more than the weasel! They all got a real fright when Tammylan so suddenly clapped his hands!

"Oh, Tammylan — you *did* make me jump!" cried Penny crossly.

"Well, I was only just in time," smiled the wild man. "Another second and Master Weasel would have pounced on the fascinated blackbird — and you didn't want to see him do that, did you?"

"Oh no!" said Sheila. "Goodness, what a strange performance! Fancy a weasel doing that, to get his dinner."

"He doesn't often do it," said Tammylan. "But I have seen one do it two or three times before, usually in a place like this, where there is plenty of bird and animal life around. And he nearly always catches somebody!"

"Well, he didn't that time!" said Penny. "But I know how that blackbird felt, Tammylan — I just couldn't say a word or move a finger. All I wanted to do was to watch and watch and watch!"

The weasel had gone—but it wasn't very long before they heard of him again! A high, shrill squeal came from behind the hedge, and all the children jumped.

"He has caught a rat," said Tammylan. "I expect it's the one I saw a few minutes ago, stalking a little vole."

It *was* a rat. The weasel struggled with the strong animal for a minute or two and then managed to bite it at the back of the neck. That was the end of the fierce rat. The weasel dragged it off to eat.

"Well," said Penny, who didn't very much like seeing or hearing anything killed, "I'm glad it was a rat and not a little vole or bird! I just don't like rats!"

When it was time to go home Sheila and Rory proudly carried their antlers. They held them above their heads as they marched into the farmyard and Uncle Tim was most surprised to see them.

"Well!" he said. "I never know what you are going to bring back with you—squirrels—hedgehogs—antlers! It's a good thing there are no hippos or giraffes in our woods, or Tammylan would make you a present of one of those, I'm sure! And what your Aunt Bess would say to that I really can't think!"

XXIII

PRESENTS – AND AN UNEXPECTED VISITOR

As the days grew shorter and colder, the children saw much less of their friend. He had moved now from his summer tree-house and was in the cave. He had made a big willow-screen to place over the entrance to his cave, to keep out the cold winds when they blew, for the winter days were bitter. It was a cold winter, and Aunt Bess didn't like the children to go wandering over the windy fields too much.

"You look so fat and well, all of you," she said. "I don't want you to get colds or coughs just before your parents come home!"

The children were going to spend Christmas at Cherry-Tree Farm, for their parents were coming straight there. They thought it would be marvellous to spend Christmas there, and have Aunt Bess's home-made Christmas pudding and mince-pies, tarts, and fruit.

"We'll all help to decorate the house," said Rory happily. "We can get berries of all kinds, and I know where there are plenty of holly trees."

"We simply *must* see Tammylan before Christmas," said Benjy. "He will love to see how Scamper has grown, and what a beauty he is."

"I wish I could take Prickles with me," said Penny, who was very fond of her quaint pet. "But he is asleep now, and I know he won't wake up in time. He sleeps all day and night in this cold weather!"

"We ought to give Tammylan a present," said Rory. "He has been such a brick to us, and all we know about the birds and animals is because of him. What shall we give him?"

"He doesn't seem to need much," said Benjy. "He lives on so little, and he doesn't think a lot of the things that most people like. It's no use giving him a pipe, or a cigarette case, or ties, like we give Daddy."

"I know what Penny and I can give him," said Sheila. "A blanket that we will knit ourselves! We will make about a hundred little knitted squares, join them all together, work a nice edging round, and give it to Tammylan to cover himself with on a cold frosty night! He loves gay things, so we will choose the brightest, warmest wools we can find!"

"That *is* a good idea!" said Rory. "I wish Benjy and I could think of something good too."

"Couldn't we make him a low wooden stool that he could use either to sit on, or as a small table?" said Benjy. "He did say once that one day he must make himself a stool."

"Oh yes! That's a fine idea!" said Rory. The boys were learning woodwork at the vicarage, and so it was easy to set to work on a stool. Benjy meant to carve a little pattern of squirrels all round it, to remind Tammylan of Scamper.

So the children were soon very busy. Sheila and Penny sat at night knitting one square after another. If they made a mistake they undid it and put it right. Whatever they gave Tammylan must be quite perfect.

The boys began the stool. It was low and sturdy, made of some pieces of old oak that the vicar had given them. They worked hard on it, and when Benjy sat trying to carve tiny squirrels round it, like Scamper, he felt very happy.

"You know, all this sort of thing is much nicer than

going out to parties and shows and cinemas," he said to Rory. "Things we do here seem to matter, somehow. Oh Rory, shan't you hate having to live in a town again?"

"Yes, I shall," said Rory gloomily. "But we'll have to go after Christmas. Penny cries every night when she thinks of it."

"Well, if I wasn't going to be twelve next birthday I'd howl too," said Benjy, digging at the wood in his hand. "Oh well — it's no use grumbling. We've had a glorious time, and it's coming to an end."

Christmas came nearer and nearer, and at last it was Christmas week. The children's parents were to come the day before Christmas, so there was great excitement. Presents had to be made and bought. The farmhouse was decorated from top to bottom. Aunt Bess made six enormous puddings and a hundred mince-pies, to say nothing of the biggest Christmas cake that the children had ever seen.

"Can we go and give our presents to Tammylan?" asked Penny one day. "It's a lovely cold frosty day, and the sun's out, and we'd just love a walk to see old Tammylan, Aunt Bess."

"Very well," said her aunt. "Wrap up warmly and go — and you can ask Tammylan to come to Christmas dinner, if you like."

"Oooh, good!" cried all the children. They packed up the blanket and the stool and set off. The air was cold and crisp, and their cheeks glowed with the frost. It was lovely to be out on such a morning.

Tammylan was in his cave, doing something that he put away quickly when the children came.

"Hallo!" he said. "I *am* glad to see you! My goodness, Benjy, how Scamper has grown! He's a bonny squirrel

170

now, and I can see you look after him well."

Scamper jumped to Tammylan's shoulder, and sat there, brushing the wild man's ear with his whiskers. He loved Tammylan.

"We've brought you our presents for Christmas," said Penny. "Look—Sheila and I made this for you to keep you warm at night!"

The girls undid their parcel and Tammylan stared at the brilliant blanket, made so lovingly and with such care.

"It is simply beautiful!" he said. "I love it very much. I shall use it every night, Sheila and Penny. You couldn't have made anything that pleased me better. Thank you more than I can say!"

171

He caught up the knitted blanket and swung it round his shoulders. It suited him very well.

"You look like an Arab chief or something," said Sheila. "Rory, you give your present now."

So Rory and Benjy undid the stool. Tammylan sat on it at once, and it was just right for him.

"Did you really make it yourselves?" he asked. "You are more clever than I thought! Who did these squirrels round the edge? You, I suppose, Benjy! You have done them beautifully. It is a lovely present—sturdy to sit on, and beautiful to look at—just what a stool should be! Many many thanks, children!"

They were all pleased at Tammylan's delight. They could see that he really was overjoyed at their kindness.

"Well, seeing that giving presents seems to be the fashion, I will give you what I have made for *you*," said Tammylan. "Here is my present for you—and like you, I have *made* it!"

He took a covering of heather off a little ledge—and there, arranged on the rocky shelf was a whole set of beautifully carved animals! They were made of wood, and Tammylan had carved them carefully and deftly himself, in the long winter evenings, by the light of his candle.

"Tammylan! Oh, Tammylan! They are all the animals you've shown us!" said Penny joyfully. "Here's the otter with his flattened tail—and the badger—and the weasel we saw in the autumn—and the stoat, with his longer tail."

"And here's Scamper!" cried Benjy, taking up a carved squirrel the very image of Scamper. "Oh, how do you carve them all so well, Tammylan? I didn't know you could do this work."

The children picked up the wooden animals and looked

at them carefully. They were all there—the hedgehog, the mole, the shrew, the vole, the otter, the rabbit, the hare—the snakes, the lizard, the toad, the frog—it was marvellous!

"I was just finishing the fox," said Tammylan. "He is really the only animal I have never properly shown you. Did you know that the hunters are out to-day, hunting the fox? I heard the horns this morning."

"Yes, so did I," said Rory. "And I saw the fox-hounds, too, and the hunters in their scarlet coats."

"*Pink* coats, Rory," said Sheila.

"Well, they looked scarlet to me," said Rory. "Listen—is that the horn?"

"Yes," said Tammylan. They all went to the cave entrance and looked out. Away in the distant fields they could see the bright coats of the huntsmen, and could hear the baying of the hounds.

"They've found a fox," said Tammylan. "I hope it isn't my old friend. He has gone through many a hunt and has always escaped by using one of his tricks—but he is getting old now, and is not so fast on his legs. I wouldn't like the hounds to get him."

The hunt came nearer. The children could hear the cries of the huntsmen and the excited barking of the dogs even more clearly. Rory began to shiver with excitement. Benjy and Penny hoped the fox would get away.

"*Why* must he be hunted?" said Penny.

"Because he does harm to the farmer's poultry," said Tammylan. "Poor old fox—he can't help his nature—look Penny, look Rory, there he is! Coming up our hill!"

The children looked to where Tammylan pointed. They were trembling with excitement. They saw a long red body with a bushy tail running up the hill, keeping beside a row of bushes. As they watched the fox, he doubled

174

back on his tracks, ran to the pond, plunged into it and swam to the other side. Then he climbed out, shook himself, and ran off the other way.

"Now you see how clever a fox is, when his enemies are near," said Tammylan. "He ran back on his track, and entered the water to break his scent. Ah—here he comes again—round the hill. He's coming here!"

Sure enough the fox *was* coming to Tammylan. The children stared in excitement. The hunted animal was panting painfully. His tongue hung out, he was wet from head to foot, and his whole body shook with his breathing.

"He's almost done for," said Tammylan. "Come on in, friend!"

The fox went into the cave, pushing by the astonished children. He flung himself down at the far end, and panted as if he would burst. Tammylan put the big willow screen across the entrance, and went to the fox.

The children went near too. The fox had laid his head on his front paws. His eyes were swollen and red, and his tongue still hung out. His breathing was terrible to hear, for his body seemed as if it must break with it. The sound filled the whole of the cave. He had run for miles and miles that morning, with the hounds just behind him.

Penny burst into tears. "I can't bear it!" she sobbed. "Make him better, Tammylan!"

"I can't do anything for him just now," said the wild man gently. "He must just lie and rest. I only hope the hounds will not come here."

As he spoke there was a terrific baying down the hill, and Rory rushed to peep out of the willow screen at the door. The hounds were smelling round, trying to track the scent of the fox, which had suddenly come to an end where he had doubled back on his tracks. Soon they picked up the scent on the track to the pond. But there the scent was broken.

"I hope they don't go all round the pond and pick it up again," thought Rory. "What shall we do if the hounds come here? There is nowhere for the poor fox to go. I won't give him to the hounds, I won't! I know he eats Uncle's hens when he can get them—but who would throw a poor tired creature like that to the dogs? I couldn't, anyway."

The fox lay panting in the cave, too tired even to raise his head at the sound of the baying. He was with Tammylan and that was enough for him. There was safety wherever the wild man was.

Rory and Sheila watched the hounds sniffing about the hill. The huntsmen had come up now and were talking to one another, wondering where the fox had gone.

"It's no use wasting time here," said one huntsman to another. "He's gone to earth. We'll go round Bell Farm and see if we can start up a fox there. Old Henry said there was a young one round there who would give us a good run. Come on. Call the hounds."

And, to Rory's enormous relief, the hunt moved off down the hill again, to join the rest of the horsemen in the valley. The hounds went too, their tails waving like tree-tops in the wind.

"They've gone!" cried Rory and he went to Tammylan. The fox was better now. His pants were slower, and he lay more easily. He looked at Tammylan with red eyes.

Tammylan put down a drink for him, and the fox lapped eagerly.

"Well," said Tammylan, "I said that the fox was the only animal I hadn't yet shown you—and now, here he is! See his lovely bushy tail, and his fine thick red-brown coat! He is a beautiful creature. He has a good burrow—what we call his 'earth', not far from here. He will go to it and rest as soon as he feels well enough. I don't believe he could have run a yard more to-day."

"What a good thing he knew you and your cave!" said Benjy.

"Yes," said Tammylan. "He has often been here and knows me well. Poor old fellow—I am afraid you will be caught when you are hunted the next time."

"I don't want him to be," said Penny, daring to stroke the fox. He took no notice at all, so she stroked him again.

"And now I will just finish doing the fox I was carving for you," said Tammylan. "Then you shall wrap up all the animals and take them with you."

He made two or three strokes with the sharp knife he used—and then stood the figure of the fox beside the others he had made.

"It's lovely!" said Penny. "Bushy tail—sharp ears—just like him! Oh, Tammylan, it's a beautiful present you have made for us. Thank you very, very much."

Tammylan wrapped up all the wooden animals and gave them to Benjy. "A very happy Christmas to you all," he said.

"Oh, Tammylan, I nearly forgot—will you come to Christmas dinner with us?" asked Rory.

Tammylan shook his head. "Thank you," he said, "but I have already asked several of *my* friends here for Christmas! I hope to have the squirrels—and a few rabbits—and maybe the hare!"

The children stared at Tammylan and imagined the cave full of his friends on Christmas Day. They half-wished they could be there with him, too, instead of at Cherry-Tree Farm!

"We'll come and say good-bye before we go home," said Benjy. "We shall be going back to London after Christmas. It's very sad."

"It is indeed," said Tammylan. "Now look—the fox wants to go. We will go with him. Maybe he will show you his 'earth'!"

The fox had staggered to his feet. He stood there, his body still trembling from his long run. He went to Tammylan and licked the wild man's hand, just as a dog licks a friend.

"He's your wild dog, Tammylan!" said Benjy. "It's a good thing for him that he knew he would find safety here!"

The fox went to the entrance and tried to push past the willow screen. Tammylan pushed it to one side and the red-coated animal slipped out. The children followed him. He went slowly, stumbling every now and again, for he was worn out. All he wanted now was to lie in his "earth" and sleep for hours.

Round the hill he went until he came to where dead bracken stood. He pushed through it and disappeared. Tammylan took the children to the middle of the bracken and showed them the entrance to the fox's den. It was a well-hidden hole. Benjy knelt down and peered into it.

"Pooh!" he said. "It smells!"

"I expect it does," said Tammylan. "Sometimes the fox makes his 'earth' near the badger's sett—and the badger hates the smell of the fox so much that he leaves his home and makes another one!"

"Well, good luck to the fox!" said Benjy. "I hope he sleeps well! Good-bye, Tammylan—and a happy Christmas to you!"

"And thank you ever so much for the lovely set of animals!" said Penny. "We'll often look at them and remember the real live animals we made friends with this year."

"And I shall sit on my new stool and wrap myself in my gay blanket—and remember the nice animals who made them for me!" laughed Tammylan. "Good-bye!"

XXIV

THE BEST SURPRISE OF ALL!

Christmas at Cherry-Tree Farm was lovely. To begin with, the children's father and mother arrived the day before—and you should have seen how they stared at the children in the greatest surprise!

"But these can't be our children!" cried their mother. "They are twice the size! And so fat and rosy!"

"We *are* your children!" said Penny, hugging her mother. "Oh, Mummy, we've had such a glorious time here—but it's lovely to see you and Daddy again."

That was a very exciting day indeed, for what with welcoming their parents, preparing their presents for one another and wrapping them up, and hanging up their biggest stockings, the time simply flew past.

"I shall never never get to sleep to-night, I know," said Penny. "I know I shan't."

But she did, and so did the others. They all took a last

look at their stockings, hanging empty on the ends of their beds, and then they fell asleep.

In the morning, what an excitement! The stockings were full from top to toe, even Rory's, who, big boy as he was, wouldn't stop hanging up his stocking as long as the others wanted to hang up theirs!

Penny had a marvellous doll, that sang a little song when she was wound up at the back. Benjy had a wonderful present — a cage with two blue and green budgerigars in it! They were beautiful birds, and kept rubbing their beaks against one another, and chattering quietly. Benjy could hardly believe his eyes!

"Just what I've always wanted!" he cried. Scamper, the squirrel, was most interested in the budgies and sat on the top of the cage, chattering to them. They didn't seem to mind him at all.

Sheila had a work-basket on a stand, all complete with scissors, needle-case, cottons, silks, wool, buttons, hooks, eyes, and fasteners. There was even a silver thimble exactly the size of her middle finger. She was simply delighted.

Rory had an aeroplane — a magnificent one that flew a very long way. Then, of course, there were their presents to each other, and the presents from their uncle and aunt. Really, the bedroom looked like a shop by breakfast-time!

They all had their Christmas dinner in the middle of the day, and Rory had three helpings of plum pudding.

"You'll be ill, Rory," said his mother anxiously.

Aunt Bess and Uncle Tim laughed. "What, Rory ill because he has had three helpings of plum pudding!" said Uncle Tim. "You don't know the Rory of Cherry-Tree Farm, my dear — did we tell you of the time that Rory had five helpings of Bess's raspberry tart and cream?"

"Don't tell tales of me, Uncle," said Rory. "Really, I'm not greedy, but Aunt Bess does cook so well!"

Everyone admired Tammylan's wooden animals. Daddy thought they were really marvellous.

"That fellow could make a lot of money if he really went in for this sort of thing," he said, picking up the carving of the badger. "This is quite perfect."

"Tammylan doesn't have even a penny in his pocket," said Benjy. "He's just a wild man. Golly, wouldn't I love to see him at this very minute—having Christmas dinner in his cave with rabbits round his feet—squirrels on his

shoulder—and the hare somewhere about too—and maybe a few mice around!"

When Christmas was over, with all its good food, its gaiety and laughter, its fruit and crackers, a horrid sad feeling settled down inside each of the children.

Now the time was really near when they must leave their beloved farm. Rory and Benjy were to go to boarding-school, and Sheila and Penny were to have a governess. The lovely free days were coming to an end.

But that year of surprises had still one more surprise in store for them! It happened when the children's parents were talking about the boys' schooling.

"I don't see how we can possibly keep up our house in town, with money so scarce, and the children's education so expensive," said Mother to Aunt Bess. "And I do wish, too, that we could keep them more in the country, because the life does seem to suit them."

Then Uncle Tim said an unexpected thing. "Well," he said, putting down his paper, "why don't you and John take up farming, as Bess and I have done? John was brought up on a farm half his boyhood, and if he buys a good farm, he won't do too badly. It's in his blood!"

Mother stared at Uncle Tim, and the children held their breath.

Their father looked up and laughed.

"What, start farming at my age?" he said. "After being in business for twenty years!"

"Yes, and that business is making less and less money each year!" said Uncle Tim. "Now listen, John—there's Willow Farm in the market, and a fine farm it is too. Take your money out of that business and put it into the farm. Come down and live there, and work it yourself. I'll help you. It's only five miles from here, and Bess and I would be glad to have you for neighbours."

There were shouts from the children, squeals and shrieks. Benjy did a sort of war-dance round his father, and Penny jumped up and down as if she were a bouncing ball. Rory and Sheila got all mixed up with one another, and altogether the room sounded rather like the monkey-house at the Zoo.

"Well, really!" said the children's father in amazement. "Have you gone mad? First Tim bursts this extraordinary idea on me — and then the whole family goes mad!"

Aunt Bess began to laugh. She laughed till the tears ran down her cheeks. The children's father looked so astonished and the children so ridiculous.

"Oh, John!" said Aunt Bess, wiping her eyes. "It may seem an extraordinary idea to you — but, really, when you come to think of it, it's very sensible. You said yourself that it's only a matter of time till your business fades away — well, you love the country, and you know farming — so why not begin now instead of waiting till your money's all gone? Then there are the children! I never saw such a set of weaklings as they were last April. Look at them now — see what a country life has done for them!"

The children's parents looked — and then they looked at one another. Neither of them wanted to go back to London. And after all, there were the children to think of. They had always been ill and pale till now. And Willow Farm was a heavenly place, with wide-set fields, silver streams, fine old barns and a comfortable farmhouse.

"Well — we'll think about it," promised the children's father. "The boys will have to go to boarding-school, but it would be good for them to come back to the farm for holidays. Yes — I'll think about it."

He did think about it — and he bought Willow Farm!

The news came the day before the two boys went off to their boarding-school, and they were wild with delight.

"We shall come home to Willow Farm at Easter!" yelled Benjy, hopping about so violently that Scamper was jerked off his shoulder. "Oh, I don't mind going off to school now — I shall have Willow Farm to look forward to. We'll have our own cows and I shall milk them. We'll ride our own horses! We'll keep our own pigs and I'll have a piglet. We'll have hens and ducks and geese! We'll . . ."

"And oh, what will Tammylan say!" cried Penny. "We *must* tell him! We *must* tell him!"

"Let's go now, quick!" shouted Rory. "Goodness, this is the best news we've ever had in our lives!"

So off they rushed to tell Tammylan, their friend. There we will leave them, running over the frosty fields to find the wild man, and to tell him of their wonderful plans for Willow Farm.

"Willow Farm! Willow Farm!" sang Penny. "Oh, what fun we'll have at Willow Farm!"

They certainly will — but that's another story!